The

SOMEDAY
SUITCASE

Also by Corey Ann Haydu

Rules for Stealing Stars

Eventown

The
SOMEDAY
SUITCASE

COREY ANN HAYDU

KATHERINE TEGEN BOOKS
An Imprint of HarperCollins Publishers

Katherine Tegen Books is an imprint of HarperCollins Publishers.

The Someday Suitcase
Copyright © 2017 by Corey Ann Haydu
All rights reserved. Printed in the United States of America. No part of this book may be used or reproduced in any manner whatsoever without written permission except in the case of brief quotations embodied in critical articles and reviews. For information address HarperCollins Children's Books, a division of HarperCollins Publishers, 195 Broadway, New York, NY 10007.
www.harpercollinschildrens.com

Library of Congress Control Number: 2016949691
ISBN 978-0-06-235276-7

Typography by Carla Weise
19 20 21 22 BRR 10 9 8 7 6 5 4 3 2
❖
First paperback edition, 2018

To best friends everywhere,
and the magic they bring to our lives.
And to my magical friend Julia.

A PERFECT DAY WITH DANNY

I am twisted up like a pretzel with my eyes closed in Danny's backyard. It's so sticky hot that I'm desperate to untwist, but that's not how you play the statue game. It is two summers ago, and we have been playing the statue game every single afternoon, so I'm an expert on the rules.

"One. Two. Three!" Danny yells at the top of his lungs, like the whole neighborhood needs to hear.

I open my eyes and he does too, and there he is, twisted up like a pretzel, just like me.

"Another!" I say.

"That's three in a row," Danny says, grinning and unpretzeling.

"Let's see if we can do four."

We stand straight up. I brush a strand of sweaty hair off my forehead, and Danny wipes the back of his neck.

"One. Two. Three," I say, and we close our eyes at the same time. With our eyes closed, we each find a shape for our bodies to make. This is how the statue game works. The goal is to make the same shape, without seeing each other. The goal is to wonder at how our best friendship is the world's closest best friendship. The most special. The most beautiful. The most magical.

I raise my arms to the sky and split them into a V. I can feel the part in my hair getting burned, but I don't care.

"You ready?" Danny asks. We have never failed at the statue game. I wait, breathe, think about the grass tickling between my toes, and concentrate on now-invisible Danny. I always know what shape he's making, and he always knows what shape I'm making. I lift one knee, certain that he is doing the same.

"Ready!"

"One. Two. Three!" Danny yells, so loud I'm sure his father, Ross, who is working inside at the kitchen table, can hear.

We open our eyes. We both start laughing. We both are reaching up to the hot Florida sun. We each are balanced on one leg. Danny's having trouble balancing. The leg holding him up is wobbly and he's sticking his tongue far out, like that will help him stay upright. He looks goofy but happy, which is the number one best combination possible.

"Having some trouble?" I ask. I am always better at balancing. Danny gets too distracted. The key is to look at one spot, a little ways in the distance, but Danny likes to look everywhere, all around, taking in every single thing. I am focused on seeing one thing perfectly, and Danny likes to try to see everything all at once. I like watching him try to stay still.

"I'm doing great," Danny says, even though we both know he's not.

"I could hold this pose forever," I say. "Should we stay like this for a while?" I lift my knee even closer to my chest and focus on one yellowing blade of grass.

"Yep. I'm very comfortable," Danny says. His standing knee wobbles. His body sways. He topples to the ground and we laugh so hard our eyes water, even though it's hardly the funniest thing that's ever happened to us.

It doesn't matter. "You two will laugh at anything," my mother's always saying when we're sputtering and doubled over in the kitchen or the pool or one of our neighboring backyards.

And she's right, we will.

"Another!" I say, knowing we will once again find the same shape in the darkness.

Because Danny and I are always a perfect match.

In fifth-grade science, we're learning about the way the world works.

Danny thinks we're learning about fish and flowers, but that's because he's only listening to every other sentence as usual. It's only the third week of fifth grade, and he's already having trouble focusing.

He passes me a sheet of paper ripped out of his notebook. Notes from math class are on one side, and he'll be kicking himself later for losing them, but when I take a closer look, they're not quite right anyway. I'm better at math and science and Danny's better at English and social studies, and together we manage to do pretty well at everything.

The other side of the paper he hands me is set up for a game of Snowman. There are dashes across the bottom, each dash representing a letter in a word I'm supposed to guess. Whenever I guess a letter wrong, Danny draws a part of a snowman—its round head or carrot nose or branch arms.

Danny never completes the snowman.

Sometimes it takes me a few guesses to get my first letter right, so he'll make a headless figure or a snowman with no face and a missing arm. But that's it. Because after I have one letter figured out, I know the whole word.

It is one of the many things I can rely on in my friendship with Danny, like the statue game. I glance at his paper even though I'm eager to listen to Ms. Mendez, who has a glint in her eye like she's going to reveal all the wackiest bits of the world to us, and I don't want to miss that.

There are six dashes on the paper. I guess a *c*, and Danny draws a large circle, a sturdy bottom for a snowman. I guess an *o*, and Danny smiles and writes an *o* in the second slot. He grins. I stare at the dashes. If I can find the word quickly, he'll let me focus on the rest of class without bothering me. He knows it's my favorite part of every day.

Danny's words are always related to something going on around him, so I know the clues are in how he's currently feeling or objects directly in his line of sight. This one's easy,

5

though—he's used the same word a million times before. I fill in the rest of the dashes.

Boring.

I roll my eyes at him. Science class is anything but boring. Danny wiggles his eyebrows in response, and I can't help laughing. Danny's eyebrows always make me giggle.

"Something funny, Clover?" Ms. Mendez asks. Her glasses have fallen from the top of her nose to the bottom, and they look like they could crash to the floor at any minute.

"No, Ms. Mendez," I say.

"Why don't you repeat to the class what I just said about symbiosis?" Ms. Mendez says.

It's not a word I've heard before, so I can't even guess. I let my foot find Danny's shin and give it a tiny but serious kick.

Ms. Mendez lets me sit in silent embarrassment for exactly ten seconds. Then she clicks her tongue and writes the word on the board.

Symbiosis.

I love science words. I love how when I hear them they don't mean anything at all, and moments later they mean more than any other word.

"Symbiosis," Ms. Mendez says, and I think from the way she says it that she likes the word too. She can be strict, but I don't mind because she is the world's best teacher. Danny may think it's all boring, but I think everything out of her mouth is magnificent. I straighten my back, waiting to hear what sort of treasure this new word holds. "It refers to a relationship where two organisms or creatures are benefiting from each other and surviving together. Because of each other. In symbiosis, each organism does something the other one can't do for itself, and they live off each other. They're dependent on each other."

Danny's kicking his chair with the heels of his beat-up sneakers, and behind me Elsa is humming something very quietly under her breath. Across the room, Brandy is looking out the window and squinting at the sun.

But for me, the world stops.

I've loved a lot of science—from gravity to evolution to the organization of the planets around the sun. It's all pretty amazing as far as I'm concerned. But I think I will find symbiosis the most beautiful of all.

"One of the more familiar symbiotic relationships is between flowers and bees," Ms. Mendez says. "Bees survive by eating the nectar and pollen from flowers, and flowers survive when those same bees drop some of the pollen on other flowers, which makes seeds, so that more flowers can grow. Each being has what the other one needs. That's one example of symbiosis. We'll be talking about more examples over the next few weeks. Symbiotic relationships can be found all over nature. Especially under the sea."

I am gripping my desk so hard my fingers start to hurt, that's how excited I am. I am finger-hurting excited to learn more.

I look to Danny, because sometimes my excitement is contagious and he'll stop calling something boring and start thinking it's awesome. I expect to see his pouty-lipped, squinty-eyed concentrating face, or maybe just another sheet of notebook paper covered in bored-Danny scribbles. But instead his eyes are watery and unfocused, and there's a hunch in his shoulders that is making his body into the wrong shape. It is not a Danny-shape.

I raise my hand, but I should have shouted out because before my hand is all the way up in the air, Danny has slumped over and hit the ground.

Danny always tells me I'm too polite and that it's okay to be a little brazen sometimes. Danny likes fancy words like brazen, instead of bold or rude or obnoxious. This one time, he's right; I should have been more brazen.

Everything is wrong. Danny is meant to be upright and smirking and fidgeting and leaning back in his chair so it wobbles a little. It's frightening, to see him on the ground instead.

I leap out of my chair and hold my breath.

"Everyone give him some room. Elsa, go get the nurse. Paloma, get some water from the fountain. Brandy, *please* step away from him." Ms. Mendez puts her hands under

Danny's head and her ear to his chest, and I sink onto the floor next to them both. She doesn't ask me to move away and give them space; I think she knows I wouldn't be able to. "He fainted, Clover," she says, looking at me very closely. "Has he ever done this before?"

I shake my head and try to remember every time Danny's ever been sick. There was a long night of him puking in my downstairs bathroom after eating Mom's terrible microwaved salmon, and the time he broke his ankle jumping off the swings. And the last few months he's had a stuffy nose and a sometimes cough that his mom says are probably allergies.

"Did he eat enough at lunch?" Ms. Mendez asks. She is relying on science even now. I decide I want to see the world the way she does—filled with facts and explanations and scientific experiments that answer all the questions that seem impossible to answer.

I scrunch up my brain to make it remember everything.

"He had two cheese sandwiches and a cookie. He mixed all the juices together and drank them really fast. Could that be it?" Danny called it rainbow juice, and some of it came out of his nose, he drank it so recklessly.

Paloma comes back with a cup of water and Elsa drags the nurse in by his hand and everyone else settles back to talk about whether or not this means the rest of science class is canceled. Danny's eyes start to open, and I take a hurricane-strength breath.

The nurse comes down to Danny's level and pushes me and Ms. Mendez aside.

"Clover?" Danny says, when the nurse asks him how he feels.

"Clover?" he says, when the nurse asks if Danny knows where he is.

"Clover?" Danny says, when the nurse asks if Danny can stand up.

"I'm here," I say. I step in front of Danny, and at last he smiles.

"What happened?" he asks me, even though I don't have those kinds of answers. I promise myself that the next time he asks, I'll know for sure.

"We'll figure it out." My heart is still beating fast, and Danny looks small and unusually timid on the floor. I keep expecting him to jump up and grab my shoulders and tell me it was all a Danny prank.

He doesn't jump up. He doesn't even sit up.

I sit on the ground next to him and hold his hand. It's cold and wet. It doesn't feel like Danny's hand.

"I'm sure it's fine," I say.

"What happened?" Danny asks again.

I would do anything to have the answer.

2

Dad's hot dogs are always a little burnt and his hamburgers are always a little bit raw, but I never care. The food isn't as good when Dad's around, but everything else is better. Dad is a truck driver, so he misses a lot of Sunday dinners when he's on the road. Last Sunday, Danny's dad, Ross, made bacon cheeseburgers and sweet potato fries, but all I could think about was how much better it would be if Dad were wrapped in an apron, flipping the burgers too early and opening a bag of greasy chips.

I was right. It's better when Dad's here.

"Burger, sweet pea?" Dad asks. Danny, Jake, and I are playing a complicated game of tag on the lawn, and I'm scared to stop for even a moment, so I call out "Both!" and forget to say please or thank you or anything else.

"Me too!" Danny echoes. He's running just as fast as he always does, so I know for sure he's fine.

"What about you, Jakey?" Dad calls to my six-year-old brother. Jake yips a nothing answer. I don't know what Dad takes that to mean, but he doesn't make Jake repeat himself. He knows—we all know—how important the game of tag is to Jake. Making up complicated tag games is one of the things Jake likes to do best. And when Jake is happy, we're all happy. His moods are big and buzzy and contagious.

Danny and I aren't supposed to let Jake win—Mom says it's important for Jake to get used to both winning and losing—but we always do anyway. When Jake wins, he jumps up and down and hugs everyone, even Danny's parents, Helen and Ross, who he's never been a hundred percent comfortable with.

Today's game—Dizzy Tag—involves spinning around in circles before chasing each other. It's the clumsiest tag, but not the messiest one. The messiest tag is Ketchup Tag, which involves each of us being armed with a squeezy bottle of Heinz and aiming for different body parts every round.

Jake tackles me and it hurts to fall in the grass, but in the good way.

I'm It.

"One! Two! Three!" Danny and Jake count in unison while I spread my arms and start spinning. I have to spin until they count to twenty. It used to be ten, but we all got too good for a count of ten.

When they get to twenty, I try to run but I keep tripping over myself—my body won't listen to me to stay upright. I bet there's a scientific reason for why turning in circles makes your limbs all sloppy and silly.

Danny and Jake are cracking up and the air smells like charcoal and the sky before it rains and melting cheese on burgers. All delicious and familiar. Getting dizzy makes me forget all about Danny's fainting the other day. Being dizzy clears my head right up, and I'm laughing too and reaching my arms out for either Jake or Danny. I hope my dad's watching through the smoke.

"Gotcha!" I yell when I finally tag Danny. He stumbles against the big palm tree that started growing in my yard but leans over so far that its top is in Danny's yard. We love that tree, and the way it isn't Danny's or mine, but ours.

We both lean against it for a moment. It's a good tree to lean against, to meet under, to try to climb even though palm trees aren't very good for climbing.

When we play tag or hide-and-seek or kick the can, the tree is safety and home base. If you are touching the tree, nothing bad can happen to you. That's what we decided.

I keep my hand pressed against the tree, and Danny does too.

Just in case we need a little extra luck.

Jake always knows the second dinner's ready, and he takes our free hands and pulls us off the tree. We're all three breathless, walking across the lawn to sit with our parents under the big blue umbrella. The parents stop talking as soon as we get to them, and we're supposed to pretend not to notice. Usually it means they're talking about something like putting Jake in a new special school or how to help Danny do better in math class or why I don't have enough confidence. They think we don't hear these snippets of conversation, but Danny and I hear enough to make sense of the secrets they think they have.

Today they've been talking about Danny's fainting, I'm sure. They look worried, even though my parents specifically told me not to worry.

"One hamburger and one hot dog for each of you," Dad says, handing out shiny red plastic plates and burgers that are too big for their buns.

"I need mayo and mustard and ketchup and pickles and onions and one tomato slice," Jake says. "No lettuce."

"We know, honey," Mom says.

"How long did it take for the doctors to figure out what was going on with Jake?" Danny's mom asks. She

14

and Danny's dad started letting me call them Helen and Ross almost two years ago, on my ninth birthday. Mom thinks I'm too young to call adults by their first names, but I love it.

Mom and Dad look at each other. The serious conversation is always supposed to stop when the kids come back to the table. I grab an extra handful of chips and Danny stuffs almost the entire hot dog into his mouth at once. Jake organizes his toppings like he's an architect perfecting a burger building. There's a long silence where Mom and Dad look to us and back to Helen and back to us again.

"I think we all figured it out pretty quickly," Mom says. "With a few missteps." She is half whispering. Not enough for us not to hear, but enough for us to know we're not supposed to hear.

"Maybe it's nothing," Helen says.

"It's nothing!" I say, even though I'm not supposed to join the conversation.

I know not to worry—if anything were wrong with Danny, I'd know, the way I know what shape to make when our eyes are closed and what word to guess during Snowman. But Helen has a strained look on her face and hasn't touched her food. It's not like her. She usually finishes hers first, and we all joke that she should enter a hot-dog-eating contest.

I don't like that today is different. I don't like that she's breaking the rules.

I know how everyone at this table likes their cookout food. I know the sounds they make when they take an extra-delicious bite and whether they open their mouths when they chew. I know what toppings they like and how many chips they eat per burger and whether they burp openly (Jake) or behind a napkin thinking no one can hear (Mom). I know who is the messiest (Ross) and who eats the most (Helen and Dad). So I know when something's off.

Something's off.

Ms. Mendez says good scientists are observers first.

"Remember that time Clover fell asleep at Disney World?" Dad says. He has a big smile and a burger in each hand. His brow is sweaty because he's the only one not completely under the umbrella. Tomorrow he'll have a burn, and Mom will shake her head and tell him he looks like a tomato. She'll tell us not to follow Dad's example, and she'll make him take an extra-large bottle of aloe lotion on his next drive. "She took a snooze on a roller coaster. We took her to the doctor, since it was so odd. They said maybe she was just tired." Dad laughs, and when he laughs, it's really more of a bellow.

Sometimes I miss him even when he's right in front of me. I want to record his rough laugh and the way he can make any conversation feel lighter, easier.

"So not to worry," he says, when he's laughed himself out. "Stranger things have happened!"

"I feel great, Mom, I told you," Danny says, and I know he's not lying because when Danny lies he leans to the left, and he's sitting up nice and straight now. "I was just bored. Clover will tell you. We're learning about flowers in science. I couldn't take it."

"I don't like how flowers smell," Jake says.

"Flowers are one of Jake's things," Mom says. Jake has a lot of what Mom calls *things*. Things that bother him or things that he has particular opinions on. Things that cause tantrums or things that have to be done a certain way. Things he needs.

I don't have very many things, except for Danny. Danny is a thing I need.

"They're one of my things too, I guess," Danny says. "Maybe I shouldn't have to go to science class anymore! Just to be safe!" Danny's fingers are covered in ketchup, and he scoots closer to his mom and wiggles them in her face. She laughs. Like my dad, Danny can make any situation lighter, sillier, simpler. It is one of my top ten favorite things about him. A lot of the things I love about Danny are things I love about my dad, and that works out pretty well, since Danny's always around and Dad's in his truck a

17

lot. Danny helps fill in some of the empty spaces.

Danny turns his ketchup fingers on Jake, getting a drop on Jake's nose. Jake squeals and dips his own hands in mustard and wiggles right back. Danny is great at riling Jake up and I'm good at calming him down, so whatever Jake needs, Danny and I have it covered.

Danny coughs and Helen shudders like it's coming from her own body.

"Take it easy, honey," she says. She doesn't like when Danny gets too rowdy. Sometimes I think it would be hard to be Helen, and not much fun. "Maybe we should head home soon. What do you think?"

"What I really want to do is learn how to use the grill," Danny says to my dad. He grabs a spatula. "Will you show me?"

"Oh, honey, is that safe?" Helen asks. She has always been a worrier, but she's even more of one today. Danny wrinkles his nose and ignores her again. It's not very nice, so I smile at Helen and ask her if she wants more lemonade.

Helen says thank you but doesn't drink much of it. Jake guzzles his down. A few minutes later, Danny turns around, grinning, holding a plate with a single hot dog on it.

"Look, Clover!" he says. "I'm the new grill master!" Dad and Ross are always fighting over who is the "ultimate grill master." "You want to be the lucky one to eat it?"

"I think I'll wait and have your fifth or sixth try," I say.

"The boy's a natural," Ross says, and I think they're both trying to make Helen relax, smile, enjoy the day. "Takes after his old man."

"You want to do some grilling too, Clover?" Dad says.

I'm not dying to learn how to grill, but I want to be near Danny and all the joking around, and I sort of want to get away from Helen and her nervous fingers and sad eyes.

Danny coughs again. It's a rocky sound, like something's stuck inside him. He smiles and opens his mouth to say something, but more coughing comes out instead. He bends at the waist and coughs into his hands, and I pat his back but I'm not sure it helps.

Helen rushes to his side and Jake starts asking a million questions that no one can answer, but when we don't answer, he just asks them more loudly.

Eventually, Jake covers his ears. He doesn't like the sound of the cough. Neither do I.

"It's no big deal," Danny says. "It's allergies, like you said."

"That's not what allergies sound like," Helen says.

"I've heard something's going around," Mom says.

"Stop!" Jake yells, and I'm sure Danny would like to, but he doesn't. He takes a big breath, like that might calm it down, but it only makes the cough louder.

I can't stop looking at the way his shoulders shake from the force of it.

"We're going home," Helen says, finally getting her way.

"Too much tag," Ross says, and I know if Ross is joking, it's probably okay.

"Never too much tag!" Danny says with a big Danny smile. The cough slows down a little and he looks to Helen, hoping she'll let him stay. She shakes her head and pulls on his arm, leading him from our lawn to his without another word.

Danny's first hot dog ends up on the side of the grill, abandoned.

Usually hot dogs and burgers and lemonade and the rules for tag are the most important parts of our Sunday.

But today is different.

There is a big life-size outline of Danny in front of me, but no Danny.

In art class last week we paired up and traced each other, and today we're meant to start working on filling in the big empty space. Ms. Fitch says we can go straightforward and draw dresses or pants or little bow ties and capture our subjects' faces. But she encourages us to be more creative and paint souls or feelings or personalities.

I don't really know what that means, which is why Danny is good at art and I'm good at science, and I need him here to balance me out.

But Danny is spending the day with different doctors, so I'm here without him.

"All he had was a cough," I said this morning, and Mom nodded and Dad said something about how Helen would take Danny to the doctor for a bug bite.

"It didn't sound good," Mom said, but she said it under her breath, so I think I wasn't supposed to hear.

I don't feel right without Danny. I get quiet and there's no one around to make me talk; I get tired and there's no one around to wake me up. At lunch there was pepperoni pizza, and I didn't have Danny there to eat the toppings so that I could just have the bread and sauce, the way we always do it. It looks gross to slide pepperoni and cheese off your pizza and keep it on your plate, so I ate the pizza, toppings and all, and now my stomach hurts.

"This unit is about how we see others and how we see ourselves," Ms. Fitch says. She has very short brown hair and a kind smile. If I could be anyone in the world, I think I'd be Ms. Fitch. She is the best artist I've ever seen, and she always finds something nice to say about my usually sloppy projects. "So we'll work on your portraits of each other, and then we'll transition into self-portraits. It's one of my favorite units."

Elsa and Levi are next to me, excitedly talking about what they're going to do to fill each other in.

"Give me mermaid hair!" Elsa says. "And I want glasses. Give me glasses."

"Draw me in a baseball uniform," Levi says. "Or make my insides all green and gross."

"Draw me a huge heart!"

"Give me robot feet!"

"I don't want to be wearing a dress, okay?"

"I want purple hair."

I miss Danny.

The outline of me lies next to the one of Danny, but there's no one here to fill mine in. I get a little nervous at the idea that it will stay empty.

"What's your plan here, Clover?" Ms. Fitch says. She's wandering the room, looking at the first steps everyone's taking, but I haven't taken any.

"I don't know what Danny would want," I say.

"That's okay, he'll figure out what he wants when he draws his self-portrait. You can draw what you want today." Ms. Fitch has a singsongy way of talking that I like. When I reply, I singsong right back by accident.

"Danny might be out all week," I say. Mom told me this on the ride to school this morning, after she got off the phone with Danny's mom. She said it in a scared voice like she knew I wouldn't like hearing it. When I asked what was wrong, and if a cough was really that big a deal, and if the fainting had to do with the cough, Mom shook her head and said sometimes we have lots of questions but not a lot of answers, and this was one of those times. I almost tell Ms. Fitch about that whole conversation, but I'm still working it through in my head. I'm not ready to talk about it out loud yet.

"Well, you'll be able to get a lot of work done while he's out this week! He'll have something wonderful to come back to," Ms. Fitch says.

"What about me?" I ask, trying not to get upset. "If Danny is out all week, who will color me in?"

Ms. Fitch tilts her head. She looks sad.

"Well. That's a very good question, Clover. Let me think on it, okay?"

"Sure," I say. I want to move away from my outline so I don't have to keep looking at how empty it is. "I just think I deserve to be colored in too."

Ms. Fitch brings her hand to the place where I'm pretty sure her heart is beating under her skin. "Of course you do."

She pats my shoulder before moving on to talk to Elsa and Levi. They make her laugh right away, and her laughter and their laughter make me feel lonelier. I miss Danny so much my fingers tingle and my ears ache and my toes curl.

I wonder which doctor he's with and what they're telling him and why Helen was so scared.

I take a red crayon. It's Danny's favorite color, so I should give him a red shirt or something. I hover over his outline and can't think of a single thing to draw. I want to write *get better get better get better* and *I miss you I miss you I miss you* all over his face.

I put down the red crayon and find a purple crayon and a yellow crayon and a light blue crayon.

And because it's what's on my mind and because it's something to do and because Ms. Fitch says sometimes art is about the things that are beautiful and sometimes it's about the things that scare you, I draw this little bruise he got when he fainted the other day. I noticed it when we were playing tag—it was small and bluish and on his elbow, which he must have hit on the way down. It was a regular Danny bruise in every way, except the way he got it.

Next I draw Danny's eyes, but I draw them closed like they were when he fainted. I make the lashes long, which his are, and his lids pale, which they are.

I can't draw a cough, but I can draw an open mouth, and I do just that.

It's a weird combination—the little bruise, the open mouth, the closed eyes, but it's everything I am scared of right now.

"Danny sleeping?" Elsa asks, leaning over to take a look at what I've done. Her hands are covered in glitter, and she has patches of glue on her arms.

"Not really," I say. I sit next to the outline of Danny,

and there's still a half hour left of class, but I can't find any energy. When I get tired during the school day, Danny sneaks me a Hershey's Kiss or tells me a joke and I wake up a little. When I'm mopey, Danny distracts me with games of Snowman or buys me a special snack at lunch. We get each other through every day. Danny always forgets pencils and I always have a full pack of twelve; Danny gets in trouble and I talk him out of it; Danny's always late and I always save us seats because I'm early.

"You okay?" Elsa says. She wipes her glitter hands on her jeans, and streaks of shiny gold and shinier purple are now all over her pants. Instead of looking messy, it looks great. I bet by tomorrow it will be a whole new trend, taking over the school.

She sits next to me, near Danny's feet.

"Oh yeah, just trying to figure out what to do next."

"What's this?" Elsa says, touching the bruise on Danny's elbow. I don't know how to answer because I don't know what it is or why it matters so much, but it does. It also matters that I don't have a bruise on my elbow. We used to get bruises in tandem. It always made our parents laugh. Danny would have a bruise on his right elbow and I'd get one on my left. Danny would scrape his left knee and I'd manage to cut my right.

When we got pinkeye, we had opposite infected eyes.

But my elbow isn't bruised one bit.

And I'm not coughing or sneezing. Or fainting.

I don't think Danny's ever had a cold without me. I don't think I've ever had a fever or a cough or a sniffle without him having one too.

"Something's wrong with Danny," I say. I don't know why I say it to Elsa. She's nice but not my good friend or anything. I guess she asked like she really wanted to know, and it feels good to say something to someone after a whole day on my own.

"Yeah, he's out today, huh? I hate when Levi's out sick." Elsa looks back at Levi. It's hard to imagine them as best friends. Elsa has long, curly red hair and big blue eyes and is amazing at art class, which is one of the coolest things anyone can be as far as I'm concerned. Levi is quiet, with glasses and short hair and a mumbly voice. He is coloring in the Elsa outline with gray marker right now, and even I know how wrong that it is. Nothing about Elsa is gray.

"I don't know how to be me without Danny," I say. "I'm not as me-ish without Danny."

Elsa looks at me hard. I thought maybe she felt the same way about Levi, but I guess not, because she doesn't nod or say *yes totally me too* or anything. Instead she walks over to my outline, the one that's not colored in and might never get colored in if Danny doesn't get back soon, the one that looks a little like how I feel right now anyway: empty.

She grabs the glue and the silver glitter and draws a heart on the outline where my real heart would be.

And like that, I have a glittery silver heart.

"That's better," Elsa says, grinning before returning to Levi.

It's not what Danny would have done, but I like it anyway.

The concrete pool on the edge of town is depressing, but Danny loves it, and when Danny loves something, it turns magical. Danny is good at making things seem different than they are.

On Saturday at the pool, I don't tell him how much I missed him all week at school. I don't tell him that I messed up our vocab test and that I almost fell asleep during social studies and that I kept bumping my shoulder on door frames because I forgot he wasn't walking through doors with me.

"Get in!" he calls from the water, but he knows I won't. Instead I sit on the edge of the pool and watch him swim. He looks like a fish. He looks happy.

Today's a good day. I have a new bathing suit and it's yellow, a color I love and Danny hates. He wrinkled his nose when he saw it, and even that made me feel good. There aren't very many people at the pool, and the ones who are here aren't paying any attention to us.

"So everything was fine with the doctors?" I ask. Mom told me not to talk to Danny about the doctors; she said it was rude and we should just be kids and have fun. Dad's on the road for a while longer, so I don't know what he thinks, but I bet he'd tell me that Danny and I can talk about anything at all because that's what best friends do. Mom and Dad don't agree on lots of things, but I think they like it that way. They have this goofy look they both get on their faces when one of them says something the other disagrees with. Like it's all an inside joke.

Danny's parents don't get that look when they disagree. Ross mostly shrugs and Helen scrunches her face and the house turns quiet. Danny says it's weird that I notice that kind of thing, but I know that everyone in the world has something they're really great at, and noticing stuff is what I'm really good at. I'd rather be good at gymnastics or painting or singing, but you don't get to choose what you're good at.

Danny hasn't answered me yet. I notice that, too.

"Hey! The doctors! You being gone all week! You're coming back to school, right?"

"Come in the water and maybe I'll tell you," Danny says. He splashes me and I kick water back in his direction, but I don't go in. "I'm fine, Clo. This is the best I've felt all week."

He didn't tell me how badly he'd been feeling all week. I have a bunch of questions that I don't really know how to ask.

"So what'd they tell you?" I say, since I can't figure out the other words I want to say. I'd like more details, so that I know why a cough and his fainting is such a big deal. I had a cough for a week last year, and I only spent half an hour at the doctor.

"They told me I'm amazing," Danny says, and he does a perfect backflip underwater.

I know that's not exactly what they said, but I don't push it. I want to relax into the sunny day and my yellow bathing suit and the ridiculous noises Danny makes when he's trying to swim extra fast across the pool.

"Let's list everything we're going to do next summer," Danny says, even though school just began and summer ended only a few weeks ago.

"But—"

"Make our own Popsicles." Danny kicks his feet, and more water hits my face. It's nice and cool and feels so good I almost want to jump in too. It feels like summer in Florida most of the time, but it almost never is.

"Sure," I say. I kick my feet around too. When Danny

helps me swim, I hold on to him around his waist and I do the kicking and he does the paddling and we move like we're one person and not two. But I don't want to do that today. Mom told me not to. She said that might be too much strain for Danny after the week he's had.

"Disney World," Danny says.

"You know that won't happen," I say. Disney World isn't so far away, but Dad says it's very expensive so I don't think we'll ever be able to go back.

"If you could go anywhere in the world, where would you go?" Danny asks. We know each other well enough that he should be flat out of questions, but he never is. It's one more thing I love about Danny. That he is curious about me in an endless, infinite sort of way. That he is cataloging my answers and making me feel like a more legitimate person. If I can answer all his questions, maybe I'll know exactly what kind of girl I am.

I am a girl who is almost eleven and likes cats.

I am a girl who eats hot soup on humid days and is a really good big sister.

I am a girl who has three pairs of red sneakers and never throws away my science notebooks.

I am a girl who is good at noticing things other people miss.

I am a girl who Danny knows very, very well.

"You know the answer," I say, because whenever it's extra hot and our air conditioner breaks, like it always seems to do on the hottest days, we talk about where we'd like to escape to. On those days, even Danny can't make Florida seem magical.

"Antarctica?" Danny asks.

"Antarctica," I say, picturing penguins and snowfall and the way I imagine my nose would feel in the freezing-cold air.

"I don't know if we'll ever get there," he says, and it's strange because that's never what Danny says. He looks sad for the length of one eye blink; then he fills his mouth with water, flips onto his back, and spurts the water up and out like a whale. I marvel at how Danny can stay on his back, floating like that, for hours. His legs never even sink and the sun in his eyes doesn't bother him, and I guess the strange, chemical taste of the pool doesn't either. "What's the number one thing you wish your parents would let you do?" he asks then.

"Like, stay up late?" I say.

Danny rolls his eyes and kicks his legs in the water like he's throwing a tantrum at my lack of imagination. He has lists of things he wants to do, but I like to make lists of what we've already done, our Perfect Days together. I like things the way they've been. I wish my dad didn't have to go on long trips in his truck and I wish Jake could go to school with me and Danny instead of his special school and I wish my hair was as curly as Elsa's and I wish my drawings were as good as Ms. Fitch's, and I wish I lived in snowy mountains instead of in sticky Florida, but mostly I'm happy with how things are.

Like today, all I really want to do is sit by the pool while Danny floats and chats away. And that's exactly what we're doing, so I'm pretty lucky. I don't even want to go to Antarctica today. I want to be right here.

"You didn't finish the summer list," I say because it's my job to keep Danny on track and it's his job to make sure we get a little off-track, sometimes.

"We should hike," he says. "And go to another pool. Some fancy pool somewhere. I'm sure we know someone with a fancy pool."

"Like, everyone at school," I say. Danny and I are the least fancy people in a town with a lot of fancy people. Everyone we know has a pool.

It's okay. We have each other instead, and it's way better.

"I don't even remember anyone at school," Danny says. "It's been too long. I've forgotten them all."

"Not funny."

"What'd I miss anyway? I can't get behind on everything."

"Let's see," I say. "Everyone's spending a lot of time making fun of the new guy, Garrett. And everyone's obsessed with playing dodgeball at recess all of a sudden. It started Tuesday, and now it's the only thing anyone wants to do. I'm bad at it. And it hurts. Why do people play dodgeball? Hm. What else? Elsa's petitioning against casseroles at lunch. Or she's planning to, I guess. The air conditioner broke during social studies on Friday, so we got to have class in the gym. It was echoey. I liked it. And I tried to fill in your outline in art class, but it mostly wasn't very good."

Danny smiles like these are all magical bits of information, as if I'm describing a dream he once had. Or a foreign country. Something to be missed and imagined and pined for.

I can't believe it was ten days ago that he fainted. It feels like it's been a year.

"You'll be back Monday, right? It's not like you can go to the pool but not to classes."

"Probably," Danny says. "They said it's not contagious. And look at me, not coughing all day!"

"So that's it?" I ask. I hold on to that *probably* tight, like it's a raft. "Everything's back to normal now?"

"Biking," Danny says, and like that, we're not talking about school anymore. "I think we should get really into biking next summer."

"Fun," I say. But there's no way we'll do it. Once the temperature is over ninety, it's hard to do anything but stay inside or take lickety-split trips to the pool. And the temperature is always over ninety in the summer.

Danny nods, but his left leg starts to sink. Then his right.

Danny is the best swimmer I know.

I leap into the water, dive deep down under to lift him up from below.

Danny is sinking.

I'm not a good swimmer, but that doesn't matter right now. I make my body move the way Danny's does—strong and confident and not scared at all.

I look over to the lifeguard, but he's too busy looking at his biceps. I try to yell for him to help, but my voice won't come. It's hiding, in fear. I'm about to flap my arms and give my hidden voice a stern talking-to, but as suddenly as they sank, Danny's legs lift up and out of my hands. He flips onto his stomach and sticks his tongue out at me.

I hate Danny sometimes.

I reach for the edge of the pool and pull myself up and out. Danny climbs out too, laughing in that sidesplitting way, water coming out of his mouth, eyes shut tight with glee.

"What is wrong with you?" I yell. The very few people

at the pool finally notice us. I'm always surprised anyone's here at all, so I'd forgotten we aren't alone. The lounge chairs don't have cushions. There are always leaves caught in the filters. Even in the relentless Florida sun, the water manages to stay icy cold. The concrete burns the bottoms of your feet and the texture cuts them up.

One older woman peers at Danny from over her sunglasses, and a boy a few years older than us turns up his headphones so loud that we can hear the shadow of his music.

"The look on your face!" Danny says, laughing harder still.

"I thought your legs had frozen or something. That you were paralyzed all of a sudden." I can feel the shakiness that comes before tears. It's in my voice and my hands.

"All that splashing and waving your chicken arms! You would have made it even worse if something were actually wrong, Clover. You could have killed me, if I were actually drowning. Never be a lifeguard." He pushes his wet hair back and climbs out of the pool to sit next to me. He chuckles and his whole body shudders with the joke that doesn't feel like a joke at all.

"You scared me! It was like when you fainted! You were fine and then suddenly you weren't! Why would you do that to me?"

"It was a joke," Danny says, throwing his skinny shoulders back and his nose up in the air.

"Not to me."

"Good thing you have me around," Danny says. "You're not fun without me." He somersaults in the water, but my heart won't slow down.

Maybe he's right, but I think he'd be in trouble without me too.

⁓⁓

"Next summer I'll teach you the backstroke," he says when he's finally ready to go home. "Everyone needs a great backstroke."

I try to think of something I can teach Danny next summer, so that we stay nice and even. But I'm having trouble thinking of anything aside from Danny's sinking limbs and rocky cough and missed school days and the fact that he never actually answered any of my questions about what's been wrong with him and I have no idea whether I can stop worrying about him yet.

"Who taught you how to swim?" Danny asks, at least the twentieth Danny question of the day.

And I tell him, but he already knows the answer. He taught me how to swim, of course.

5

"What's your favorite sea creature?" Danny asks in science class on Monday, putting his textbook up over his face so Ms. Mendez can't see his lips move.

I want to be listening to her descriptions of sea creatures with symbiotic relationships, but I'm so happy to have Danny back in school, I'll answer any questions he asks. I've played six rounds of Snowman and missed probably twenty-seven interesting science facts.

"Don't say dolphin," Danny says before I have a chance to answer. "Everyone says dolphin. You're better than that."

"Sea horse," I say. I don't know anything about them, but I like their name and their tails and that they sound original enough to appease Danny. "You?"

Danny gets a big goofy smile on his face. If Ms. Mendez asks him to lower his book, he won't have time to get rid of the smile, that's how big and wide it is. "Dolphins," Danny says. "They're amazing."

I roll my eyes and smile too, but I don't have a book up, so I get a look from Ms. Mendez. I fold my lips in to show her how very quiet I can be. I kick Danny's shins, and he coughs. I worry that I caused the coughing, that I made him sick again. I look his way, though, and he's fine. His smile has shifted into a smirk, and he raises his hand.

"Yes, Danny?" Ms. Mendez says. She hasn't told him to put his book down, and I think she's only pretending not to notice that he's fidgety and chatty and not really paying attention. Maybe she's happy to have him back, too.

"May I go to the bathroom?"

Ms. Mendez nods and writes a bathroom pass for him. "Try to gather yourself before you come back in, Danny."

He nods but his eyebrows wiggle too, and Ms. Mendez sighs but not in a very angry way. I know from experience— it's not easy to stay mad at Danny.

I look at the board. There are new science words up there that I don't know, so I write them in my notebook with a promise to look them up on my own time. I also promise myself that starting tomorrow I'll be back to my regular Clover self and make sure we don't get too distracted by Danny's games and jokes. We'll go back to being Danny and Clover—Danny reminding me to have fun, me reminding Danny to focus. The week of doctors is over, and even Helen seemed calm on our ride to school this morning.

"We'll be taking a field trip to the aquarium to view some of these spectacular beings," Ms. Mendez says. There's a hooting and hollering epidemic. Everyone loves a field trip. I can't wait to tell Danny when he comes back from the bathroom. He'll pump his arm in the air and wiggle in his seat and ask a billion questions about what kind of trip it will be.

I look at the door. He should be coming back any second.

Ms. Mendez hands out permission slips and gives me an extra one for Danny without even explaining. Everyone knows that we're a pair. She writes down page numbers to look at for homework and reminds us to start thinking about our science fair projects too.

"We learn all these exciting scientific concepts that are in our world so that you see how far science reaches," she says. "And your science fair project can be about anything. Any part of the whole wide world that interests you. Maybe it's flowers or symbiosis or the sea, or maybe it's something else entirely. Electricity. Technology. Anatomy. Chemical reactions. Solar power. Any question you have about the world that you can try to answer through science."

I write it all down—the homework and the field trip date in a few weeks and the science fair date. November 8. I'll show Danny later. With me around, he won't miss anything at all.

I look at the door again. No one's there.

I watch Elsa pack up her books, and Levi cleans off his glasses, puts them back on, and straps his backpack over his shoulders. Elsa waves at me and tells me she likes my hair in a ponytail. I want to tell her I like her hair all the time, but I'm pretty sure that would sound stupid, so I say thank you instead.

"Levi and I are getting ice cream after school," she says. "You should come!" Elsa's never asked me to hang out before, and a smile surprises my face. It is a good feeling.

"That sounds fun!" I say, thinking of raspberry chocolate chip and vanilla with sprinkles and this weird basil ice cream that my mom likes. I'm about to tell Elsa about basil ice cream and how it sounds gross but it's actually sort of good, but then I remember Danny and that he still isn't here. Elsa says something else, but I don't hear her. I nod anyway.

Brandy puts on her cat-eared hoodie. I stay seated. I don't want to pack up without Danny. My book bag is always bigger than his, so I take more books and he takes the heavier ones, and it works out perfectly every time.

I stay seated even though no one else is.

A girl with black hair and big ears, a few years younger than us, comes to the door instead of Danny. She says something to Ms. Mendez that makes Ms. Mendez motion at me with a *come here* finger. I leave my books and my backpack and my favorite green pen and head to the front of the room.

Ms. Mendez puts a hand on my shoulder. "Clover, Danny's at the nurse's office and he's asking for you. I'll write you a note. Who's your primary teacher? Mr. Yetur? I'll let him know. It sounds like it'd be a good idea for you to be with Danny."

I nod.

"You can leave your things here and get them later."

I nod.

"I'm sure he's fine, but you're a good friend for being there for him."

I nod and nod and nod. But I don't understand anything at all.

Danny's on his back on a cot in the nurse's office. Mr. Purvis is mostly good for Band-Aids and temperature taking, but this time he's got his stethoscope out and is listening to Danny's heart. They both startle when I come in the door, like they were listening very, very closely to hear it beat.

"I didn't faint," Danny says.

"He lost his breath," Mr. Purvis says. "On his way back from the bathroom."

Danny wheezes, like he has to prove it to me. It's a sound that doesn't sound human. It sounds like when the washing machine is broken or Dad's blowing up an air mattress for when Danny sleeps over.

"That doesn't sound good."

"Does Danny have asthma?" Mr. Purvis asks me, like I'm Danny's mother or doctor or something.

"I told him I don't," Danny says. He tries to get up on his elbows, but it makes him wheeze more. He leans back down.

"I thought maybe Danny might have forgotten. I'll talk to his parents about it."

"Are Helen and Ross coming to get him?" I ask, already picturing another lonely lunch by myself and a depressing art class with no one to color me in.

"His mom's on her way."

"I'm right here. Don't talk about me like I'm not here," Danny says, before the coughing starts.

I move closer to him and he sits up so that I can rub his back, which my mom does for me when I have a bad cough or any sort of ache or pain. The coughing gets worse for a moment, then subsides. He takes a few deep breaths.

There's a wheeze, and another, before his breath sounds clear again.

I'm starting to really hate the sound of Danny's cough.

"Does he have bronchitis?" I ask. Danny tenses up. "He's had a cough for a while. He went to some doctors. Jake had bronchitis last year. It was mostly coughing and sleeping."

"You're talking about me like I'm not here again!"

"I'm sorry. Danny, do you think you might have bronchitis? Is that what it feels like?" I try to think about what Ms. Mendez says scientists do: they look at concrete facts and from those concrete facts come up with theories.

"Maybe," Danny says, but Ms. Mendez would say that maybe is never enough to prove a theory. "My stomach hurts. And my ears feel kind of clogged up."

I add clogged ears and stomachache to the list of Danny's symptoms in my head.

"Maybe you should go to my doctor," I say. "She's nice. She always asks what I want to be when I grow up, and she figured out Jake's bronchitis really easily."

"Keep rubbing my back," Danny says. "I can breathe when you do that."

I stop talking and rub his back. We stay like that for a while, Mr. Purvis taking Danny's temperature and blood pressure and writing down the results. I sneak a peek. I know what the temperature means—100 degrees is a little high—but I don't know what the blood pressure numbers mean. I'll have to look it up.

"Clover, you can go back to class. Danny and I can wait for his mom together," Mr. Purvis says when Danny's breaths get deeper and clearer.

"No!" Danny says. He has a twinkle in his eye that Mr. Purvis is too blind to see.

"Something hurt?" he says. He puts a hand on Danny's forehead and one on his back, shifting mine aside and taking my place.

"Everything hurts, and I don't want Clover to leave," Danny says. He puffs his lower lip out a little, so that he looks more pathetic, and his eyes go big and wide.

I'm pretty sure he's faking it, but I get sad hearing him say *everything hurts* anyway. I don't want anything to hurt.

"I think you'll be okay here with me for a few moments," Mr. Purvis says. "We don't want Clover missing class, do we?"

Danny's eyes flit to my face, and there's a hint of a smirk. He's trying to help me get out of class, and that would be nice, except he's forgetting that I have math next and I love math. We've been learning about statistics, and we get to do group experiments with coin tossing and dice rolling and talking about baseball. I might even like baseball.

My teacher, Mr. Yetur, teaches everything but science, art, music, and gym. He has a beard and wears Muppet ties and gets marker on his nose most days. I think math is his favorite thing to teach. I don't want to miss it.

I don't want to be in the nurse's office while everyone else is recording heads-and-tails ratios in spiral notebooks. I have my awesome green pen and a newfound love of the number seven, now that I've started drawing a fancy line through its middle.

It's hard to want two things at once: to be in math class and to be around my best friend.

"I really feel better when Clover's with me," Danny says. "It helps. Can't she stay?"

Mr. Purvis sighs and nods and turns his back to us. Danny grins when Mr. Purvis isn't looking, proud of doing me a huge favor. I try to smile back, but everything in the nurse's office smells like rubbing alcohol and cough syrup.

I watch the clock for Danny's mother to arrive. When she finally gets there, she looks paler than Danny.

"He's okay," I say right away to try to make the nervous look on her face go away.

"We're going to go to the special doctor your pediatrician recommended," Helen says like she hasn't heard me at all. I didn't know about any special doctors. "We're going right away. Do you need help getting up?" She puts her hand on Danny's forehead, and I take a step out the door to make room for her.

"I think it's bronchitis," I say. I try to say it like the doctor

47

would: in a serious voice with no question mark on the end.

"We'll see, Clover," Helen says, not looking at me at all.

Danny looks at the ground.

"I can't walk," he mumbles. "I'm tired."

One minute ago Danny seemed fine, but now he's so tired his eyes look droopy, like they do when we have sleepovers and try to stay up until the sun rises.

"I think I need someone to carry me," he says. I look to see if he's smirking again, to see if this is another Danny plan. He's blushing. His arms looks floppy and he's not fidgeting at all.

"I've got this, Helen," Mr. Purvis says. Danny's skinny and Mr. Purvis lifts him up easily, but it looks all wrong anyway. Ten-year-old boys aren't supposed to be carried around like babies.

I watch them go, Danny's mom click-clacking down the hall and Danny with his arms around the nurse's neck. Soon the hallways will be full of kids and teachers and jokes and dropped pencils and the smell of gum.

But not now.

Right now it's me, alone.

6

The next day, Ms. Mendez writes with red marker on the dry-erase board.

SCIENCE FAIR

Danny and I have been waiting for our own science fair since we started attending it in first grade. Danny's always wanted to build a robot and I've always wanted to do a project on how plants grow, and I figured we'd find a way to meet in the middle: a plant-growing robot; a robot that is actually a plant; a project on how to teach a robot to garden.

"It's time to pick partners. You're also welcome to work

on your own. Proposals are due on Monday," Ms. Mendez says. She doesn't have to explain much about the fair, because we already know everything there is to know about it. It's a huge all-school event that only the fifth graders participate in. The rest of the school attends, wandering around the crowded cafeteria and the playground, where all the exhibits are set up. Everyone at school votes on their favorite project, and someone wins Crowd Favorite and someone else wins Best in Show from the judges, and there are big trophies and shiny ribbons and a whole day off from the sticky classroom.

"What if our partner is out today?" I ask. Elsa and Levi look at me with sad eyes. Marco sighs like he's already tired of my sick best friend.

"She means Danny!" Brandy says, and the rest of the class giggles, because it's really pretty easy to giggle at Brandy.

"Why don't we talk about it after class?" Ms. Mendez says. Her lips are pulled tighter than usual, and it feels like something's wrong.

"Can I get an extension, though?" I ask. It's not like me. Usually I listen to what the teacher says and stay quiet. Danny's the one who asks lots of questions and interrupts and gets notes on his report card about being disruptive. I get notes about not speaking up enough. "I need an extension so

I have time to talk to Danny about what we're going to do."

"We'll talk after class," Ms. Mendez says again. And I can see it in her eyes, in the way her hands grip the marker, in the way she watches the class watch me—she doesn't think Danny will be better in time to be my science fair partner. She doesn't think he's okay.

I sink back into my seat.

I miss Danny so much I can barely hear Ms. Mendez or see Elsa mouthing *Are you okay?* to my left.

"Your project should be something you can get passionate about," Ms. Mendez says. She's sneaking glances at me to make sure I'm okay. I'm not. "Scientists care about their subjects. They fall in love with their work. Scientists aren't afraid to feel. They choose something to study that makes their hearts beat and their toes tickle and their minds whir. Be scientists."

I take halfhearted notes. The letters droop and slant down. They won't stay on the lines of my notebook. I can't think of anything to be passionate about without Danny there to push me along. Danny is in charge of passion and I'm in charge of reason, and that's how things work best.

I've lost track of what makes my heart beat and my toes tickle. My mind is not whirring at all. It's frozen.

"You want to join our group?" Elsa asks. "We're going to do a project on the weather. We're going to figure out how to predict when the rain's coming."

I think of how me and Danny and Jake are always trying to predict the exact hour of the day that the afternoon shower is going to come.

"I'm really good at the weather," I say. "I always know when the rain's coming."

"Then we should test you," Levi says. If Elsa said it, it would be a joke, but coming from Levi, it's a real suggestion. He adjusts his glasses and looks at me very, very closely, and I think he honestly wouldn't mind doing a science experiment on me.

"Maybe," I say, shrugging. I shouldn't shrug, because it's so nice that Levi and Elsa want to include me at all, but I feel all shrug-y and I can't seem to shake it. "Do you think you're allowed to do a science fair project on a person?"

"Sure!" Elsa says, and she's getting a little giggly at the idea of doing a project about me, and I'm wondering how I can tell Danny that I had to join another group because Ms. Mendez, my favorite teacher in the world, wouldn't let me wait for him to get better.

And that's when I think of it.

Danny.

If Elsa and Levi can do a project on me, I can do a project on Danny.

Ms. Mendez said to pick something you care about,

something that you're desperate to know more about, something you're passionate about.

That's Danny.

"Science is about the need, not the want, to answer life's big questions," Ms. Mendez says. She's pacing the room, watching us come up with ideas and shift into pairs and trios.

My heart lifts way up high—all the way through my throat and head and to the ceiling and beyond until it's up in the sky and landing all the way back with Danny in his bed at home, sad and sick and alone.

"You know what?" I say to Levi and Elsa. "I think I'm going to work alone. I'm going to do a project on Danny."

Elsa's face slides into disappointment that is trying to be something else. "You can't do a project with Danny," she says. "He's not here."

"Not *with* Danny," I say. "About him. I'm going to find out what's wrong and I'm going to find out what will make him better."

Levi adjusts his glasses again. "Isn't that what doctors are for?" he says.

"I know Danny better than the doctors do," I say. "If science is about caring, I'm the best scientist to do this."

I nod to myself and Elsa swallows hard, and I know they don't believe that I can fix my best friend; but I know that I have to.

Ms. Mendez reaches me last, after hearing about Levi and Elsa's weather project. Elsa waves her hands around, talking about the thunderstorms, and I think she'll have a really successful project, because it's obvious she cares so much.

"And what about you, Clover?" Ms. Mendez says. "I know you were hoping to do this with Danny, but I talked to his mom after everything yesterday, and it sounds like he might not be able to work on a science project this year. But I bet he'll assist you if he starts to feel a little better. How does that sound?"

"Actually, Ms. Mendez," I say, taking a big, preparing-myself breath, "I'm going to make my science fair project all about Danny."

Ms. Mendez's whole face wrinkles up, but she doesn't say no.

A PERFECT DAY WITH DANNY

I t's December three years ago, and we're watching winter
movies.

"Why can't it be like that?" Danny says. He gets close to
the TV, so close his nose almost touches the screen, which is
how Danny watched TV when we were littler.

"Like what?" I ask.

"I don't know. I want mittens and hot chocolate and big
tall boots," Danny says. "I want to make a snowman."

"We have mittens!" I say. "Or my dad does."

Danny pauses the movie right on a shot of a woman
in a red scarf sticking out her tongue to catch snowflakes.
"Where?" he asks.

We head into the garage, where Dad keeps his winter wear. He has to have all kinds of things for when he gets an assignment to drive up north during the winter. He keeps it all in a big box in the garage marked *Winter*, like you could find the actual season inside.

Danny opens the box, thinking winter will pop out like a jack-in-the-box, and he's disappointed for a half second to see only a puffy coat and some mismatched gloves and two bulky scarves. Then he remembers he's Danny and he can make anything exciting.

"Better get ready for the big storm," he says. He pulls a gray wool hat over his ears. It has a pom-pom on top, and I poke at it. He throws a red striped scarf around my neck and lets me wear the bulky blue coat. It feels like a sleeping bag. He pulls an itchy sweater over his T-shirt and drags me outside, even though it's seventy-five degrees out there.

He makes a pretend snowball and throws it at me. I screech, like something cold has hit my face. I don't know what snow feels like, but Dad once said it was a little like Italian ice, so that's what I picture. I lean down and make my own fake snowball, bigger and colder than Danny's. I wind up and throw it, hard. He leaps when it pretend-hits his neck.

We go back and forth, making bigger and bigger fake snowballs until we are making them so large we have to roll them instead of throw them.

"Is this what winter is like?" I ask him.

"I think so," he says, and we are both beaming from the newness. "I think it's like this, but better."

It's hard to imagine anything better than the way we feel right now—silly and sparkling and alive.

I barely notice how hot it is in my sleeping-bag coat. I barely notice that people are looking at us as they drive by. A few of them honk, and Danny and I wave like we're celebrities and not kooky kids pretending to be somewhere else.

"We're going to do this for real someday," I say, even though it feels almost real now.

Danny throws another fake snowball at my face. I screech like it's hit me in the nose.

"Promise?" Danny asks.

"We'll find winter," I say. "I promise."

A car slows down, and inside are people making pinched faces at us—trying to tell us how weird we are.

I feel bad for them, that they will never have as much fun as Danny and I do.

D anny has Band-Aids on the insides of his elbows. They're Superman ones, but I know Danny doesn't even like Superman.

Jake loves Superman. When he sees Danny's elbows, he goes crazy.

"Can I have the Band-Aids? You don't need them, right? I can have them?" Jake peels one off Danny's right elbow and I cover my eyes. We've been out on the lawn, the three of us, for an hour, but so far all we've talked about is what shape we think each cloud is and what time we think the daily Florida rain shower is going to come.

"Jake, stop! Gross!" I say, covering my eyes, but Danny only laughs.

"Hey, if Jake wants my old dirty Band-Aid, he can have it. I'm not even bleeding anymore," Danny says. "I don't have any blood left anyway. The doctors took it all."

He's saying it all like a joke, but it doesn't feel like a joke to me. I spread my fingers apart and look at Danny's skin that's been exposed. It's bruised yellow, and there's a little red dot in the middle like a target.

It looks like it hurts.

"Did they find anything?" I ask. Danny shrugs. "Are you coming back to school next week?" He shrugs again. It's been a long week at school without him. Most days it's been hard to even talk to him—he's busy with doctors or he's too tired to come to the door, or Helen's worried that I might make him sicker, somehow, with my germs.

"That means no," I say.

I don't tell him about the science fair, or what I've decided to do my project on.

Jake puts the Band-Aid on his jeans, trying to make it stick. It's not going well, but Jake's not one to give up. Plus, he loves anything Danny gives him. Jake is maybe the only other person in the world who loves Danny as much as I do.

"Can I keep it forever?" Jake asks, and I smirk, but Danny gives a serious nod. They're both in wrinkled shirts and sneakers that used to be white but are now gray. They both have tan shoulders and burnt tips of their noses, all shiny and red like little Rudolphs.

I get filled up with a warm, gooey, inside-of-a-chocolate-chip-cookie feeling.

"I hope I'm never so sick they have to take all my blood," Jake says, because Jake will say anything in his matter-of-fact voice. He doesn't notice the way I shiver in my skin from the comment. The warm-cookie feeling seeps out of me and I need answers, before I can relax.

"Come on, Danny. Tell me the truth," I say. "Did the doctors figure anything out?"

"Not yet. They said they need to run more tests. They said sometimes it's tricky to figure out what exactly is going on inside someone's body," Danny says. "I'm going to Tampa. There's a guy there."

"A guy?" I ask. "Tampa??" Danny's eyes are clouding over, and I know that means he doesn't want to talk anymore, but I don't care. And it doesn't matter that Jake is jiggling his knees and I know that means he might throw a tantrum any moment. Once I want an answer to a question, nothing else matters to me. Dad says that's why I'm so good at school, and Mom says I take after her and I'll have to watch out.

I think I just care about stuff more than other people must.

"I want to go to Tampa!" Jake says. He clings to Danny, wrapping his little hands around Danny's skinny arm. He

60

must do it too tightly, because Danny winces and unwinds Jake's fingers.

Jake turns his back on Danny. He doesn't like being told not to do something. Usually the two of them can wrestle and tear at each other's skin and hair and yelp and growl for hours. My mom calls it rabble-rousing, but there's not going to be any rabble-rousing this afternoon. I've never had blood taken before, so I didn't know it would hurt after, and the realization makes me sad. I want to wrap Danny's arm up in cotton balls and old blankets and everything soft.

"They want to do some other tests," Danny says, because he knows if he doesn't explain something about Tampa, I'll only keep asking more and more questions. "Like X-rays but more intense or something. I don't know."

"How can you not know?" I look around for something to write on, but of course there's nothing out here but our sad plastic kiddie pool and an old-fashioned sprinkler Mom lets us run around in when it's really hot, and two swings and one plastic slide that I'm too big for now, and our shared palm tree watching over us. I can see a little ways into Danny's yard, where there's a big rock we like to hide behind when there's something disgusting for dinner. There's a time capsule we buried beneath the ground by the rock, but no spare paper or pens. "Let me run inside and get a notebook," I say. "I'll take notes."

"It's not school, Clover," Danny says. He tries to tickle Jake, but Jake's staying good and mad. Danny tries to tickle me, but I need answers, not giggles. I need to start solving the problem of What's Wrong with Danny so we can start answering the question When Can Danny Come Back to School with Me?

It's bigger than the science fair. It's bigger than anything I've ever done before.

"What exactly are they testing?" I ask, even though I know Danny wants to talk about something else. I'm not letting him get away with it, though. "Why are they freaking out?"

"I keep having weird little symptoms. So I guess they're testing everything. Blood. Lungs. Heart. Skin. My liver and kidneys. Everything. Mom wants me to get acupuncture, but Dad says it's expensive, and I say the last thing I need is more needles."

He's listing off body parts and treatments and tests, but what we need is a chart and an anatomy book and a plan. I look to the kitchen window, and Danny notices.

"It's fine, Clo. I feel fine, I swear. You know my mom. She's making a big deal out of nothing."

"I have a doctor kit," Jake says, finally deciding to look at Danny again. The Superman Band-Aid is clinging to his jeans, but just barely.

"I've had enough doctors," Danny says. Jake huffs.

"Does your kit have a microscope?" I ask. Jake lies on his back and makes his whole body very stiff. Then he starts to roll, back and forth and back and forth, two and a half turns each way. We used to just roll like that down the hill behind Danny's house, but lately Jake's started doing it on flat surfaces too.

"I said no more doctors," Danny says. "Let's go in and watch a movie. Is your dad here? Maybe he'll take us for ice cream."

"Dad's on the road this week, you know that," I say. Danny always knows Dad's schedule as well as I do.

"Doesn't your mom have an ice-cream-making machine? Maybe she'll let us use it." Any other day this would be the best idea in the world. It's sticky-hot out, and late Friday afternoons are the best times of the week to come up with new things to do. A whole weekend is stretching ahead of us, and we can fill it with anything we want. I think the Florida daily shower is coming in the next ten minutes, maybe less, so it's time to move indoors.

But I don't care about any of that. I want to know what Jake's doctor kit has.

"I have a microscope, but we're not allowed to use it without Dad," Jake says. "That's the rule."

Jake loves rules.

I don't usually mind, but today we can't follow the rules.

"We need to use it," I say. "We'll look at Danny's blood. Maybe we'll see something."

Jake stops his rolling.

"The rule is that Dad has to be here," he says.

"Clover. There's nothing to see. It's blood. It's gross," Danny says. He leans back in the grass now too, so I guess he doesn't feel the rain coming like I do. Usually, we feel it coming at the same time.

I'll take a note about that, too. My science fair project is going to have so many notes I will have to pile them all into a bunch of different binders, all labeled and color-coded and scientific.

I know Danny better than any doctor ever could, and I feel so sure that if I could just see the blood they're looking at, I'd know what's happening with him. Ms. Mendez says that in science there's the world we know and the world we don't know. She says both worlds have explanations, but we just haven't figured out the explanations for one of the worlds yet. She says science knows things we don't.

Ms. Mendez says every creature has a job in the universe. My job is understanding Danny.

"I can see the rain coming," Danny says. "It will be here in an hour."

"Five minutes," I say, lying next to him, watching gray invade the blue.

Jake plops himself in between us so that he can get a glimpse of the oncoming showers, too.

"How do you know when it's coming?" he says, squinting, never quite understanding the game.

"We don't, really," I say.

We're lined up nice and tight, and with our heads so close to each other, we can be sure we're seeing the sky from the same angle. I like sharing that with them. I like knowing we're all seeing the world the same way, for this one moment.

Then it starts to rain.

8

We have to wait for Jake to get to bed before we can use the microscope. He had a great afternoon and evening with Danny, and trying to get him to break the rules would have ruined that for him. There would have been a tantrum and Mom intervening and Dad getting an upset phone call from Mom while he's on the road and the whole family having long talks about the way rules have to be flexible sometimes.

Instead we ate Mom's summer pasta and made extra-sweet lemonade and played Monopoly for hours before bedtime. No one won, which is almost always true of our Monopoly games.

But as soon as Jake's asleep, I beg Danny to go get the microscope with me.

It's the only expensive toy we have, which is why Dad put such strict rules on it. It's kept in the family room, in a cabinet, still nestled inside the box it came in. I'd forgotten all about it, but Jake never forgets about anything.

"This is stupid," Danny says. I promised his mom we'd go to bed early since he's supposed to be getting his rest, but he seems perfectly fine, so I push away the little bit of guilt I feel about it. We set the microscope up on the living room floor.

"I'll feel better if I can see what they're seeing," I say.

"There's nothing to see," Danny says. "Look how well I'm doing." He does ten jumping jacks, and I worry that the noise will wake everyone up. Danny is not good at staying quiet.

"They saw something." Since Danny won't answer my questions, I'm going to start making statements instead.

Danny doesn't disagree. He does stop doing jumping jacks, though.

"We just need a drop of blood. We'll put it in between these two slides, and we'll be able to see some stuff. It won't be perfect, but it'll have to do." I know that in science you're supposed to do everything perfectly, but we don't have all the tools that doctors have, so a messy blood sample will have to do. I remember Dad teaching us how to use the microscope two years ago—we looked at pieces of grass and moldy bread and some of Danny's hair.

I know enough to know how to do this.

"You want me to give you blood?" He says it in a vampire voice—breathy and replacing *want* with *vant* and singing the words a little.

"One drop," I say.

"Seriously, Clo?" I guess Danny thought this was all some big joke, but I'm so super serious. I've never been so serious. I stole a needle from Mom's sewing kit, and I washed the slides to make sure they are shiny and clear for the sample. I washed my hands, too.

Danny looks pale, and I can't stop thinking of all the days of school he's missed. No one misses that much school if they're not really sick. Danny keeps saying he's fine, but it's a lie, because if he was fine, he'd be in school, and I'm smart enough to know that.

"I need to see," I say. "You have to let me see." I don't mean to cry, but I start to anyway.

Danny can't stand it when I cry.

I hand him the needle.

"You have to stop crying first," he says. He holds it between two fingers, and I can tell he's really starting to hate needles. I look at his exposed elbow again, at the yellow-and-blue bruises from where they took blood, at the tender way he bends the joint, like it hurts whenever he moves.

It makes me cry more.

"Clover. You have to stop," Danny says. "Think about penguins on motorcycles and cats in top hats." He knows I love animals pretending to be humans. The tears dry right up. I can't help but laugh.

Danny pricks his finger. He doesn't make a noise, but his face sort of hiccups. I capture one perfect red drop on the glass slide.

That's when I remember I hate blood. I almost drop the whole thing. There's a little bubble of blood on Danny's finger still, and he covers it up with a tissue.

It all makes me queasy.

Ms. Mendez says science isn't always pretty. She says it isn't all neat and clean.

"Science is for the brave," she says.

I hate blood, but this is important. It's for science. It's for Danny.

I press a second slide on top and put the little blood sandwich under the microscope like they do on TV. Already I feel like a real scientist. I play with the focus and try to use the microscope the way Dad taught us: with my eye open, not scrunched against the lens.

At first all I see is a blurry mess. But I breathe and relax and move the focus very, very slowly. I'm patient.

"What are you even looking for?" Danny says. He's fidgety, and he keeps hopping from one foot to the other. There's a whine in his voice, which comes whenever he's sleepy.

Then I see it: dozens of little pink circles, all the same size. They look like jellyfish floating in the water. They look as slow and sleepy as Danny did right after he fainted. They're transparent, like the shiny, soapy bubbles we blow in the backyard. I smile. I'm the only person who knows that Danny loves blowing bubbles. Jake loves it too, and Danny always offers to do it with him.

I push Danny to the microscope to show him the beauty of what's going on inside him. He stops breathing as he peers down through the glass.

"It's pretty. It's like a whole universe in that one drop," I say, already eager to see more.

"Yeah."

"Everything's okay," I say.

"I don't really see anything, Clover," Danny says. "I'm not sure you did it right." He moves away from the microscope and flops onto the couch, and I think he's about to pass out there. When Danny's tired, he falls asleep quickly. We can be mid-conversation or in a car or at the pool, and he's all of a sudden sleeping, with no warning at all.

I want one more glance at the drop of blood. I want to see again, with my own eyes, that everything's okay.

I lean over the eyepiece, like my dad taught me to. I focus. I blink and relax. I smile at how every single thing in the world is made up of millions of other, smaller things. I don't care that Danny said he couldn't see anything. I see what I need to see.

Each circle is the same size and shape. Perfect pink bubbles.

Except for one.

I didn't see it at first, or maybe it simply hadn't bobbed into view, but there is one circle that is a little bigger and a little more square-looking. I focus the lens. I squint.

It's all wrong, that one cell in the midst of all those perfect Danny cells.

I jump away from the microscope like if I stop looking at it, it will disappear.

~ ~

I don't want to tell Danny, but when I try to sleep, all I can think about are all those pretty pink bubbles and that one not-quite-right cell that doesn't fit in and shouldn't be there. I toss and turn and try to imagine unicorns and rainbows and sheep jumping over walls, but nothing works.

Danny snores on the floor next to me, bundled in a

sleeping bag. He likes sleeping on the floor better than in his own bed, he says.

I wake him up when I can't take the not-sleeping for a minute longer.

"You fell asleep," I say.

"You woke me up," he says.

We both laugh a little. Everything's sort of funny after midnight.

"I saw something scary in the microscope," I say.

Danny moves to sitting up and looks at me very seriously.

"You're not a doctor, Clo," he says. "And that microscope isn't the fancy kind they had at the hospital. I don't think you really saw anything, okay?"

I think about Danny's words and the thing I saw. Everything was a little blurry and fuzzy and indistinct. He could be right. I might have seen nothing at all. Maybe everyone has some sort of square cells in their blood.

Ms. Mendez says that a good scientist listens to other scientists. A good scientist doesn't get distracted by their own feelings. I try, try, try not to get distracted by all my fear. I know Danny is at least a little bit right.

"They're not fixing you fast enough," I whisper. It's the real, true thing. More true than whatever I saw or didn't see under the microscope.

"Mmmm," Danny says, already drifting off, too tired to tell me that they will fix him, of course they will.

So I stay awake and take notes on everything I know about Danny and science and mysteries and hope.

I'm up all night.

List of Danny's Symptoms

- Fainting
- Weak arms
- Weak toes
- Stuffed-up ears
- Runny nose
- Nightmares about fish
- Nightmares about aliens
- Nightmares about the way we all feel lost in the dark
- Sweating
- Aching
- The color of his face turning from wheat to white to a terrifying almost-blue
- A cough that sounds like a garbage truck
- A cough that sounds like the wind
- A cough that sounds like he is trying not to cough

9

Dad forgets towels when he brings Jake and me to the pool on Sunday.

"I'm out of practice," he says with a Dad grin. I have missed Dad grins and Dad laughs and Dad burgers and Dad talks. He's been gone for two weeks this time, since the day after our last cookout, and I'd forgotten the shade of his skin (mostly burned pink) and how exactly we talk to each other. I feel nervous around Dad whenever he gets home from his long trips, and desperate to tell him everything I can possibly think of, to make sure I get it all in before he leaves again.

"That's okay! We can rent towels!" I say, a little too

excited, and wrapping my arm around Dad's arm like a vine. Jake's having a *don't touch me* day, so he walks ahead of us but stops in his tracks when he hears we'll be renting towels.

"Those towels are dirty," Jake says. "We can't use those."

"They're fine," I say. "They clean them with all kinds of chemicals, I bet. Right, Dad?" I stare up at my father. The sun hits his blond hair and turns it to gold.

"Sounds right to me, smarty-pants," he says.

"Fine. We can rent them when we get my floaties," Jake says.

Shoot. Dad won't like that.

Jake knows how to swim just fine, but it started making him nervous, so Mom put floaties on his arms and promised him a scoop of ice cream for every half hour he stayed in the pool.

I know she hasn't told Dad yet. There are some things we don't tell Dad. "Because it's easier," Mom says, which I think means that she's sad he's not here more often.

Jake and I have never been allowed to use floaties. Dad says the only way to learn how to swim is to jump in and trust that you'll float. I wanted the floaties. It's part of why I never learned how to swim well. Danny acted as my floaties, and that's still how I like to swim best.

But Mom lets Jake break the no-floaties rule.

"It's different for Jake," Mom says, and I guess I know that it is, but it bothers me sometimes anyway. It's hard to always stay smiley about things that feel unfair.

"You don't use floaties, Jake," Dad says, heading up to the rental stand.

"Yes, I do," Jake says. I want to fade away. I hate these moments—when I have to explain something to Dad about the new way our family works when he's gone. It makes me miss him even more. I stay quiet.

"You absolutely do not, Jakey," Dad says. "It's okay to be scared, but you're a good swimmer. You can trust your own arms to hold you up."

"First we put on sunblock, then we rent floaties, then we get in the water, and after half an hour I get a scoop of ice cream," Jake says. He doesn't sound upset, just matter-of-fact, like he's reading a grocery list. Dad looks to me.

"Clo?"

"I'm not using floaties," I say.

"What about Jake?" Dad scratches behind his ear like a dog. It's something he does when he's getting upset but doesn't want to show it. I do the same thing when I'm trying not to show my feelings.

I wish Mom had remembered to tell Dad about Jake and the floaties before we got here. I don't want Dad to be upset on one of his few days with us. Mom says when

Dad's home we have to work to make memories that he can carry with him in his pocket on the road. I'm worried that if today goes badly, Dad will leave again in a few days with empty pockets.

"Jake's been using them some," I say, because there's no way to lie with Jake around. "He likes them. I'm sure Mom meant to tell you. Or probably she was going to get him to stop doing it after a few days." My voice is shaking, and Dad hears it too. He softens.

"Hey, it's okay. It's all right. I missed a little change in the routine. That's okay. We'll get Jake some floaties. I'll remember for next time. But make sure you two don't stop liking ice cream or burgers or singing show tunes in my truck, okay?" Dad ruffles my hair and I nod big and hard so he knows how much I mean it.

Dad gets towels and floaties and we set ourselves up in old plastic chairs a little bit out of the sun. The chairs squeak and settle and the umbrella has a hole in it, but I like how familiar it all is. Jake jumps into the water, floaties and all, and I have a minute alone with Dad. He looks over at me and smiles.

"How's it been, Clo? Catch me up." The sun is so hot my knees and back are already slippery with sweat. The smell of chlorine is a nose-wrinkling level of strong, but this is the best part of my time with Dad. I take a deep breath, like I always do when he says this to me.

"I grew half an inch in the last month," I say. It's one of the things I've been waiting to tell Dad. I have a whole list in my head. I gather up bits and pieces from each day and store them to tell Dad all about later. I'm doing it for Danny now too, with school. My brain is working hard, trying to remember enough for me, Dad, and Danny. "And there were three days last week where it didn't rain at all, and I knew it wasn't going to rain because my ankles didn't get that achy feeling, so now I'm sure that definitely works. And we're learning about symbiosis in science class, and I think it's the most beautiful thing in the world. And I started working on my science fair project. I think it's going to be—it's a big project."

Dad looks at me like I'm a constellation he's still trying to place in the sky. I glow from how special he thinks I am.

"What else?" Dad says. He sneaks a peek at Jake, who's twirling in circles in the pool.

He sounds so curious, so serious, when he asks that I say the words I've been holding in and swallowing down and trying to make leave my mind.

"Danny's not getting better. He keeps getting worse."

Dad leans forward and grabs my foot in his hand. He squeezes. It crushes my toes a little, but it's what Dad does when he wants to say he's sorry and things will get better.

"It will be okay?" I ask in a little voice I've been hiding from everyone. "Danny will be okay?"

Dad is the only person I believe more than I believe science. If he says Danny will be okay, I'll be able to relax a little. I could add Dad's opinion to my list of notes and use it as a little piece of evidence.

I think, I *hope* that Dad's about to tell me that of course it will be okay and that I'm his brave, smart girl and that most things that seem scary actually aren't, but he gets distracted. Jake has jumped out of the water and is cannonballing back in. The few people sitting by the edge of the pool shiver and grumble in response, but Jake doesn't notice.

"Careful, Jake!" Dad says.

"Jake doesn't really like that word anymore," I say. Jake's a little like Danny, in that I know what he likes and doesn't like better than anyone else. There's a catalog of facts in my brain about them both. Danny's is fuller, Jake's is messier. It's hard to keep track, and I know Dad feels bad when he doesn't get it right, so I try to say it gently.

"What does he like?" Dad says, scratching behind his ear again.

I want to say a billion things, but we only have this one day with Dad, so I have to be choosy.

If Dad were a doctor or an accountant or a mailman, he'd live at home all the time and I'd get a million moments to tell him everything. But Dad leaves on another trip on Tuesday, and I guess he'll have pockets filled with memories, but I still won't have gotten my fill of him.

Jake screeches.

"He likes me to go in the pool with him to help him calm down. He gets upset when he's in there alone," I say. Dad nods, and I guess that means I should go take care of Jake now. He squeals an awful pig noise and makes his limbs drumsticks, beating at a rapid pace in some heavy metal band. I sink into the pool and move very slowly toward him. Other swimmers have waded away, so he has a corner of the pool all to himself and all eyes are on him. A group of girls look so angry I'm worried they'll yell at him, and that will only make it worse. I take hold of his wrists, and he bites my shoulder.

"Jake!" I yell. It doesn't hurt, but I'm shocked.

"Clover!" Dad calls out.

"EEEEEE!" Jake screams.

We are that family.

I wish all the annoyed people at the pool could come to our house and see our cookouts with Danny's family and the way Jake runs when we're playing tag, all loose limbs and big smiles, making circles around the tree we all share. I wish they could see ketchup on Dad's face and Mom's paisley apron and Danny's messy hair that somehow always gets mustard in it even though his mouth is pretty far from his forehead. I wish they could see us being a fun family under a big umbrella when the daily Florida rain comes down and the time capsule hidden in the backyard and our hiding place behind the rock.

Dad steps into the pool too, but it won't matter; it's me who Jake needs when he's like this.

"Let's play the stay-still game," I tell Jake. "The statue game. Let's be statues in the water! Do you think you'll win?"

The statue game is different with Jake than it is with Danny. With Jake, the statue game is about calming down, stilling the world, finding some quiet in all the chaos. With Danny it's about shocking ourselves and dancing when we match shapes for the hundredth time and falling into the grass afterward, laughing. With Danny it's about *being* the chaos.

"I always win," Jake says. He sticks his tongue out in concentration and puts his arms above his head and stays so still it's as if his arms have forgotten the panic they just caused in the water. Jake can be one thing and then another. He moves quickly and slows down with the same amount of focus. I guess my brother is confusing to some people, but not to me. I understand that he doesn't always know why he's upset and that he gets scared at the not knowing.

I get scared at the not knowing too. Jake and I are the same that way. We both feel best when we know as much

82

as possible. That's why I looked in the microscope and tried to make sense of what I saw, and that's why Jake wants to hear the rules of the statue game again, even though they never change.

"We both have to stay perfectly still. We are allowed to breathe and blink and that's it," I say. "Dad will tell us who moves first. Okay? Go."

The girls with the angry faces and arms relax, and Dad mouths *I'm proud of you* at me. That's probably the end of our Dad-and-Clover talk, and it will have to be enough to get me through another few Dad-less weeks.

I move my hands above my head and spread my fingers wide. Jake arches his back and puts his hands on his hips and sticks out his tongue.

We stay as still as we can for as long as we can.

⁘ ↝

On the drive home, Dad tells me there are gifts for us in his duffel bag, which is at my feet. He always brings something small back for me and Jake. Dad's truck brings oranges from Florida to Boston, seafood from Boston to San Francisco, and apples from San Francisco back to Florida. He finds little presents for us in different states along the way. This time he's brought Jake a Boston Red Sox hat. Jake started collecting hats. He likes to know the whole history behind each logo.

"I have something special for you, Clover," Dad says. He

hands me a snow globe. I have been collecting snow globes for years, and this one is especially beautiful. "That's the Public Garden, in Boston," he says. I shake it up and watch the snow whirl in the globe before covering the garden's grass.

I imagine for the millionth time what it must be like, to watch your world get covered up in white wonder. I imagine me and Danny in the garden, sticking our tongues out to catch stray flakes, shivering in the cold, instead of sweating in the heat.

"It's beautiful," I say. Dad nods and hands me another identical one.

"Thought I'd get one for Danny too," he says. Danny doesn't collect snow globes, but he loves the idea of snow even more than me, if that's possible.

And maybe I didn't get enough time to tell Dad every single thing about Danny and all my feelings, but somehow he seems to know anyway. I hold one snow globe in each hand, shaking them up for the whole ride home.

Maybe getting lost in the magic of snow globes can't cure Danny, but it fixes something in me.

～～

I don't get to give Danny the snow globe right away because by the time we get home, he's in the hospital.

10

On Monday, Elsa brings me a plastic ring with a huge purple bauble and a sparkly band. It's almost like she knew about Danny's hospital stay and how sad I've been since he went in on Saturday.

"It reminded me of you," she says, taking my finger and squeezing the ring on.

It's self-portrait day in art class. "Now that we've worked on interpreting someone else, it's time to express our inner selves," Ms. Fitch says. There are no outlines for the self-portraits, just big blank pieces of paper. "Get creative. Maybe you see yourself as an animal or with rearranged features or entirely neon pink. Whatever feels right to you is right."

Elsa scoots next to me and I worry that Levi will be jealous, but he's fine, sorting colored pencils in front of him. It's a good choice. Levi was made to be drawn in colored pencils. Elsa's outline of him from last week is colored in with blue stripes and he looks like a ship captain and not a sixth-grade boy. I can't wait to see the difference between how she sees him and how he sees himself.

I love this project, even though it hurts that I don't have Danny to do it with.

I hold my hand up and out so I can stare at the ring. "This reminded you of me?" I ask. I like the idea of a ridiculous glittering purple ring making Elsa think of me. I've always thought I'm boring and shy and too serious, but I guess Elsa sees special things in people—sea-captain-ness and purple sparkly insides.

"Danny's the fun one," I say, and Elsa looks confused.

"I wasn't talking about Danny," she says.

"No, I know, but with me and Danny—we fit together. We're like one person. He's fun and I'm responsible. He's bright colors and I'm plain colors and that's really okay. I'm not a sparkly ring."

"I know you're not a sparkly ring. But you can wear a sparkly ring." Elsa smiles, and her smile makes me smile.

"I'm sorry I didn't get ice cream last week," I say. After Danny went to the nurse, I walked around like a ghost of myself and totally ignored Elsa when she asked if I was going to come with her and Levi.

"That's okay!" she says. "You'll come next time, right? It's fun. We try to eat the whole cone before any of it melts. I usually win."

I usually get ice cream in a cup, but I don't tell her that because I'm worried she'll disinvite me and it sounds really fun. Elsa is really fun, I'm realizing. I've known her for my whole life. I've known everyone at my school my whole life, basically. She has a sweet voice and chubby cheeks and is really good in art class. I don't know why she's suddenly wanting to be my friend, but it feels good.

"Next time. Definitely," I say, and I silently hope that there's a next time really, really soon.

Everyone likes Elsa, and she likes me.

Then I remember that every day after school Danny and I walk home together and his mom makes us sandwiches and we eat them on my front lawn. We get cookies from my parents' cabinets and it works out perfectly. Danny hasn't been at school in a week, but it feels wrong to do something else.

"Girls, time to take all that wonderful talking-energy and turn it into creating-energy," Ms. Fitch says. She has the best way of scolding us without doing any scolding. We get right to work. Elsa invites me to where she and Levi are set up so that I don't have to work alone, next to the outline of Danny with his sick insides.

I'm relieved. Standing next to that outline gives me a nervous feeling in my belly that I haven't figured out the right word for yet—not quite sticky or achy or dizzy, but something else.

Elsa is making a collage of eyeglasses and eyes. I'm trying to draw my face in charcoal, but it keeps smudging and I'm not sure I know what I look like. I am not good at art class.

"I always wished I had outfits like yours," I say, when we've been quiet for long enough for Ms. Fitch to wander to the other side of the room. Levi looks up like maybe I'm talking about him. He glances down at himself, finding a blue plaid button-down tucked into khakis. He shrugs, and I think I get how he and Elsa are friends. They're different, but they have something important in common—not caring so much about what everyone thinks.

Elsa's skirt is long and flowered and her T-shirt is sort of too long, but it doesn't matter on her.

"Thanks," she says. "I try to look like Levi's mom. Have you ever met her? She's so cool." I relax. I want to be more like Elsa and Ms. Fitch, but it's okay because there's someone Elsa wants to be more like, too.

"And your hair. It's curly. I want curly hair," I say. I

don't talk about this kind of thing with Danny, so I'm not good at it yet. For instance, Elsa knows her hair is curly, so I didn't have to remind her about it. I sort of forget how to talk to people who aren't Danny. I shake my head and try harder. "Why is your self-portrait eyeglasses?" I ask, thinking Danny would be so much better at this whole talking thing. Danny knows how to make friends, and I'm good at remembering things like their birthdays and favorite colors and whether they eat meat or pork or dairy or peanuts. But the friend-making part at the beginning is Danny's domain. He talks fast and makes jokes and everyone spits up milk from laughing so hard. I try to pretend to be Danny. "You don't have glasses," I say.

I am not Danny. I'm not even good at pretending to be a little like Danny. But Elsa doesn't seem to mind. She gets this dreamy look on her face, and I can tell she loves nothing more than talking about art.

"You know how Ms. Fitch said self-portraits are about the artist's view of themselves?" Elsa says. I fall in love with her voice. It's light and breathy and sounds like what I imagine a doll would sound like. It's the kind of thing people would make fun of if Elsa were the sort of person people made fun of.

"I remember," I say.

"I think of myself as having glasses," Elsa says. She

laughs and blushes. "That sounds stupid. But when I think about myself, that's what I see. So that's what I'm doing."

"That's not stupid," I say, and feel extra sad that I chose to do my self-portrait in charcoal. Is that how I see myself? Cloudy and gray?

"It's funny yours is all dark and blurry," Elsa says. "I mean, it's cool. I like it. But it doesn't remind me of you."

"I feel sort of blurry sometimes," I say, and I'm surprised I've said it out loud. Danny's the only person I say things like that to—weird, sad things. Secret things. Things Mom would never want me to say out loud.

"Funny," Elsa says. "Like me and the glasses."

I play with the ring she bought me. I love how it shines and looks a little too big and a little too strange. Most of all I like that Elsa gave it to me. Maybe Elsa's right. I like things that are bright and fun, even if I don't feel that way inside all the time.

Elsa is my new friend, I realize.

I made a new friend, without Danny.

I feel a little proud and a little guilty.

"Can I start over?" I ask Ms. Fitch. She makes her way to me and my sad charcoal failure and hums at it.

"Why don't you add on to it, instead of starting over?" she says. "This is one layer. There can be others. I bet this charcoal you is one layer of you, and now we can find the other parts of you." Ms. Fitch says things that blow my mind a little. I want to remember this sentence and tell Danny. I write it down on a sheet of construction paper, and Ms. Fitch doesn't have to ask why I'm writing it down. "What can I bring you?" she asks.

"Glitter," I say. "Markers. Paint? Like, watercolors maybe?"

"A little of everything," Ms. Fitch says. She winks. Ms. Fitch is the only teacher I know who can wink without it seeming silly.

I fold up the construction paper and put it in my pocket with the slip of paper telling Danny about what the score was at dodgeball in gym class and what next three books Mr. Yetur is assigning us to read. I'm filled up with wanting him to be here. I'm filled up with not wanting construction-paper notes in my pocket. I'm filled up with guilt that I'm liking Elsa so much.

Ms. Fitch gathers the supplies for me, and although I'd like to cover the thing with glitter and be the person Elsa maybe sees, I start with the watercolors. I make my hair a watery yellow and add a pink halo around my head. Then I'm stuck.

I like who Elsa sees, but I don't know what I see. And I don't really know what Danny sees either.

I don't think I can know what I see without knowing what Danny sees.

Maybe I could call home sick and see him right now

and do the self-portrait on his kitchen counter.

He wouldn't be there, though. Mom said she wasn't quite sure how long Danny would be staying in the hospital. She said it with a sigh and a shiver.

"I like what you're doing," Elsa says. She's picking glue off her fingers and flipping through magazines for more images for her collage. She adds huge red-framed glasses and pointy cat-eyed ones.

"It's not . . . whole," I say. I squint at the image. It's missing glitter and bright colors, I guess, but it's missing more than that.

I don't look like me, even though my hair and my lips and my nose are right. I don't look like me even with eyes that look a lot like mine and a polka-dot shirt.

I don't look like me because I'm not me without Danny.

I pick up the charcoal again and draw a figure to the left of my face. Small. Bony. Spiky-haired. Danny.

Right away the portrait looks more complete. More like me. More like the me in my mind. More like the me I've always been.

"It's supposed to be a *self*-portrait, though," Elsa says a few minutes later when she's blowing on her collage, waiting for glue to dry. She makes a whistling noise with each blow.

"It's like you with the glasses," I say. "It's how I see

myself, right? I see myself with Danny."

"Right," Elsa says with one big nod. And I can see that she doesn't quite get it, that she thinks it's a little silly or strange, but that's okay. Danny and I aren't easy to understand. We're like science or math—it seems really complicated, but actually it's so simple and perfect and true.

Danny and I are a science experiment. We're a math equation. We're a self-portrait with two people instead of just one.

When Mom picks me up after school and asks how my day was, I'm embarrassed to tell the truth: that it was a great day.

I don't think I'm supposed to have great days without Danny.

"It was okay," I say.

"Only okay?" she says, like she knows I'm hiding a secret. I fidget. I hate lying.

"It was a really good day, Mom." I hang my head.

"Good days should make you smile, honey." She keeps trying to decide if she should look at me or the road. I want her to look wherever she needs to look to get us to Danny faster.

"I shouldn't have been doing something fun while Danny's so sick," I say.

Mom reaches over and squeezes my shoulder.

"Nothing you do can make Danny better or worse," she says. "It's not your responsibility, okay?"

I nod, but I'm not sure I believe her.

~~~

"I want your Jell-O," I say when Mom, Helen, Ross, and I are all up in his tiny hospital room. It's sitting there, all jiggly, on Danny's lunch tray, and no one can think of anything else to look at, so we're a room of people staring at Jell-O.

He laughs so hard at that one sentence that I know for sure it's been nothing but frowns and cold stethoscopes and worried whispers for days. He laughs so hard at that one sentence that I'm worried things are way worse than I thought.

"It's all I have in the world," he says. "How dare you take my Jell-O! What kind of friend are you?" He has an IV in one arm and his eyes are sleepy. He has a fever.

He is the sickest I've ever seen him. I didn't understand why he had to see so many doctors and skip so many days of school until right now, until this second right here.

I'm supposed to say something funny back, but I get distracted by the sweat on his brow, by the pointy IV and the way it glints at me, like a warning.

I ask him what his temperature is and write it down

in my science notebook, alongside my symbiosis notes. Ms. Mendez says the best scientists watch and listen and record, then think about it later. She says science is beautiful because it is a way of communicating with the world we live in.

I try to name the color of Danny's cheeks. Ms. Mendez says scientists are very specific. *Ivory with gray mixed in,* I write. *Yellowish-beige,* I write. *Sandy with a hint of fog.* None of it captures the actual color, though. *Sick-colored,* I write, and that's the best I can do.

"It's okay," Helen says, "you don't need to take notes, Clover. The doctors are doing that." Helen's talking to me the way I sometimes talk to Jake, and I think I get it now, why he hates it so much. I try to be nice because I think you have to be nice in the hospital.

"I know," I say, matching her slow, quiet, careful tone.

"You can put the notebook away, honey. We're here to hang out with Danny," Mom says.

I give Danny a look, and he gives me a look right back. He nods. "It's okay," he says. "I like when Clover helps. I need all the help I can get."

Helen sniffs. The sniff turns into a hiccup, which turns into a little cry. She excuses herself.

"You know not to say things like that in front of your mother, Danny," Ross says. He sounds tired. Danny looks tired too. There are lots of new rules about what we can and cannot say and do, and the new rules must be really wearing them all out.

"It makes me feel better to tell Clover how I'm doing," Danny says, and this seems to be enough for Ross, who nods and steps back. Mom puts a hand over Danny's hand, and we all pretend for a moment that we're not in the world's smallest, cleanest, whitest hospital room.

Danny takes a deep breath that looks like it hurts. He tells me to write down that he ate applesauce for breakfast and nothing else. He tells me how he felt at seven in the morning and at noon and that he feels a little better now, at four thirty in the afternoon, with me right next to him watching his every move. I'm monitoring the changes in the weather as they relate to his fever. (*It's raining now; it will stop soon; his fever is down from 104 to 101; the air conditioner is so strong my nose and toes are cold; the one sad window is foggy from humidity.*)

"What are the other symptoms today?" I ask, pen poised. I sit on the bed next to him, and our knees touch. Neither of us eats the Jell-O. We didn't want it anyway; we just wanted something silly to talk about.

A doctor comes in, as if the word *symptoms* calls him to action. Danny's mom comes back in too, red-eyed and puffy-faced and not really looking my way.

Danny starts coughing, that awful cough that I

sometimes hear in my head at night. He coughs so much his whole body shakes, and the bed too. He coughs so much that Helen tears up again and I think Ross wants to cover his ears.

Everyone else steps away from coughing Danny. But I go right for him. He's leaning forward, so I get my hand on his back and rub. I press down hard and keep the motion slow and smooth, right along his spine.

The hacking turns to regular coughing.

The regular coughing turns to big, scratchy breaths.

The scratchy breaths turn to regular breaths, and Danny's skin looks the littlest bit pinker and healthier.

The look on Danny's face is total confusion.

"I haven't taken a full breath in days," he says. He puts his hands on his ribs like he wants to make sure they're all there.

The doctor looks surprised too, and he gently pushes me aside. He puts his stethoscope under Danny's shirt in the back and has him take some big breaths. The doctor smiles a little, listening to the in and out.

"You sound better. Sounds like you've cleared up a little. I like to see that. Maybe we'll have some answers soon." He takes a bunch of notes. Doctors love taking notes. They scribble really fast and bite the ends of their pens. They mouth things, words that take shape but don't make sounds.

They scratch the ends of their noses with the tips of their pens and I'm pretty sure they write one thing in the notepad while saying a whole different thing out loud.

"You hear that, Helen?" Mom says. "Danny's sounding a little better. You'll know more soon." She's doing that thing where she says something positive but keeps frowning.

"I've been feeling pretty good since Clover got here," Danny says. The doctor looks up like he's finally remembered there are more people in the room than just Danny and his lungs. His eyes rest on me. They're nicer eyes than I originally thought. Shiny and grass-green.

"You must be Clover," he says. He looks less like a doctor when he smiles. "I've heard a lot about you these last few days."

"I'm trying to figure out what's wrong with him and what helps him," I say. I want him to take me seriously.

"We're trying to figure that out too. We're trying medicine and diet and rest and all kinds of things. We're running a lot of tests and watching him very closely. It seems like something's finally helping."

"Ms. Mendez, our science teacher, says a good scientist is always open to all possibilities," I say. The doctor smiles. I think I like him. I think he's a good doctor.

"We're going to figure this thing out," he says. I nod. I think he's including me in the *we*. "About time to wrap up with your visitors, Danny. I'm so happy to see some of what we're doing is working for you."

Danny's straight up in bed. He looks good.

"Maybe I'm all better now! Maybe I'm not sick anymore!" he says, but I know we have to focus on research first, then conclusions. Danny doesn't like that method. He has always had big dreams and this fizzy, fun imagination. We had an imaginary dog when we were six, and Danny's pretending made him seem almost real. His name was Rocky and he was a goldendoodle. He was big enough for us to ride on his back, and we even brought him to the dog park a few times.

With the power of Danny's imagination, it was almost like really having a real dog.

Same with our fake snowball fight. It felt real. Danny's imagination can conjure pets and weather patterns and even magical healing powers.

It's Danny's job to have big, crazy dreams, and it's my job to figure out the real world. If he's better, why? What has he been sick with? What made it happen? What's making it fade?

I want to remind him of Rocky and how real he sometimes felt; I want to remind him of all the things Ms. Mendez says about being a scientist; but Danny's almost his regular color and his breath isn't having any trouble moving in and out of his mouth. He's not sweating or shivering. He's better and he doesn't care why.

I care why.

I scribble in my notebook and try to describe everything that's happened at the hospital today and any possible evidence there is about what is making Danny sick.

"Oh, I almost forgot!" I say, going to my bag and pulling out the extra snow globe. "Dad got one for me and one for you too."

I hand it to Danny.

He holds it gingerly, like it could break. He doesn't shake it to watch the snow flutter. He lets the world, the snow, the universe inside the sphere stay still.

"There's a whole world outside the hospital," Danny says. He sounds like he's dreaming, but he's right here.

⁓

On our drive home, Mom turns off the radio, which means she wants to have a Serious Talk.

"It's not your job to fix Danny," she says. "I want to make sure you know that."

"I know it's not my *job*, but I want to help," I say. "I want Danny to get better."

"You have to let the doctors do their job, and you stick to being a fifth grader, okay? No need to be too adult. You can keep having nice days at school with your new friend Elsa.

You can visit Danny without a notebook."

Mom doesn't like when I'm being *too adult*. She has worried about it since I was little. I'm *too adult* when I'm getting up in the middle of the night to help Jake with his nightmares, and I'm *too adult* when I'm getting up early to fix Dad a few bags of snacks for his truck rides. I'm *too adult* when she catches me watching the seven o'clock news before bed, and I'm *too adult* when I ask her if we're going to be able to pay our bills this month.

"He's really sick, Mom," I say. It's the first time I've said it out loud, and my voice breaks on the words. So does my heart, because I know it's true. "Did you hear what he said, about the world outside the hospital? He's sick and he's sad and he's lonely."

"I know, Clo. I know." Mom turns the radio back on. "But you need to be a kid no matter how sick he is."

We drive by Levi's house, which isn't so far from mine. I've been there a few times for birthday parties and end-of-school get-togethers. It's a nice house, and he has a nice mother with long brown hair and lots of bracelets on her wrists. Her name is Rachel, and people say she's strange. They say it like it's a bad thing, but I'm pretty sure it's a good thing.

Levi and Elsa and a few of my other classmates are on his front lawn today with water guns and water balloons.

Everyone is soaked to the bone and open-mouth laughing.

I could be there, I think, with the bare feet and the dripping hair and the promise of a Popsicle and a sunburn.

That's what Danny meant, about the world outside the hospital. There's so much out there.

Hypotheses: Things That Maybe Help Danny

- What they feed him in the hospital (Jell-O????)
- The medicine they're giving him at the hospital
- The IV in his arm
- Danny's mood
- Hours of sleep the night before
- How much water he's drinking
- Body temperature
- Amount of physical activity
- Time of day
- The special tea Helen makes him drink some days
- Positive thinking
- Having visitors, especially me

12

Danny finally left the hospital Thursday night, so on Saturday morning I bring him bagels, even though he's had a stomachache since getting home. Three bites in, he starts to feel better.

"Bagels might be the cure," I say, and I'm joking, but I write it down anyway. The doctors tested a bunch of foods he could be allergic to, so maybe there are some foods that make him feel better, too. Ms. Mendez says it's important to entertain all ideas, all theories. "Just because something sounds silly doesn't mean it is," she said. "Great scientists don't dismiss anything."

Danny raises his eyebrows at my note taking, but he

doesn't say a word. I finally tell him about the science fair project, and he raises his eyebrows at that, too.

"I'm not an experiment," he says. He's got a half smile and cream cheese on his chin. He's saying one thing, but I can see he's going to let me do it.

"I need to take your family history," I say.

"Clover. Come on. I do tests all day, every day. When you're here, I want to relax." He scarfs the rest of his bagel and his face brightens—what was gray is pink, what looked gaunt seems full. He looks good. He looks like Danny, only a little knobbier and sleepier.

I understand. I really do.

But all the understanding in the world isn't going to make me stop trying to figure out what's happening to my best friend.

"You have to let me do this," I say. It comes out quiet and strong all at once, and that combination forces Danny to listen, I guess, because he looks me in the eyes and nods.

"Family history," he says with a big sigh. "My parents are healthy. . . ." He trails off, and that's when I know there's something he's been hiding from me.

"I know your parents are healthy," I say. "What about the rest of your family? Doctors are supposed to know everything about your whole family."

"Yeah," Danny says. "They know." He taps his foot and

looks at the remnants of our breakfast—globs of cream cheese, used napkins, black and white seeds that fell off the bagels.

"And?"

"My dad's dad was sick a lot, I guess."

"With what?" I poise my pen over my paper. Ms. Mendez says research is messy and not to worry if the pieces don't seem like they fit together. But I have a feeling I'm about to hear something that fits. I'm desperate for something simple and clear and obvious.

"They don't really know," Danny says. "Auto something? I guess it was a little mysterious. A little like what I have. My dad doesn't remember too much."

There's a pause and I have one hundred questions, easy, but Danny doesn't want to hear any of them.

"The mall!" he says, like he's only now remembered the word. "Mom said if I felt good, I could get out for a little while. Let's go to the mall!"

"What were your grandfather's symptoms?" I ask. "Did they have a name for what he had? Do they know what caused it?"

"Mom told me the word for what they think it was. It's a medicine word. I don't know what it means." Danny clears his throat. He doesn't know what the word means, but I think he doesn't like saying it anyway. "Autoimmune." He shrugs. He clears his throat again. "Sounds scary."

"I'll look it up," I say, and write down the ugly word.

"I don't want to know anything more about it," Danny says. We are opposites in this. I like knowing everything about everything, even bad things. Danny likes to know as little about bad things as possible, so he can imagine they don't exist.

I draw an enormous star next to the word *grandfather* in my notebook before we get in the car.

⁓

"One hour only," Helen says before we leave the car. Danny's asked me to put my notebook away while we're at the mall, so I'm carrying it in one of his mother's canvas tote bags. She seems to collect them the way my mother collects bookmarks and I collect snow globes.

I think each of our collections means something big and important, but I'm not quite sure what.

"That's it?" I ask, and the nervous feeling I'm getting used to swarms my heart and throat and toes. We always stay at the mall for at least four hours.

"That's all he can handle. He needs to rest," Helen says with pursed lips and no eye contact.

"It's the mall," I say, and I know that Mom would call me out on having attitude, but I don't think it's attitude if I'm stating a fact, so I keep going. "He doesn't go to school, and now he can't do anything else either?" I've never argued with Helen before. I'm not sure it's a good idea.

"I'm letting you go to the mall," Helen says. "Don't be dramatic. It's just going to be a nice short trip. That's what's best for Danny. And right now we have to do everything we can to keep Danny well, right?"

"We don't know what helps Danny feel better yet," I say. "We don't know what's making him sick. You can't conclude that the mall is bad without evidence."

"Clover," Helen says, and I can hear how sick she is of me just from the way she says my name, "you aren't a doctor."

"Of course I'm not," I say. "I'm a scientist. Ms. Mendez says scientists can be any age. Some people get fancy degrees, but being a scientist is a special way your mind and your heart work together, that's it."

Helen doesn't have anything to say to that. "One hour," she says again, instead of continuing the debate.

The mall is air-conditioned and we can get extra-large lemonades. But being together outside Danny's house or the ugly hospital room is what makes today special.

All we do for the first ten minutes is make pinched faces from the lemony lemonade and watch people, and it's the happiest I've been all week. We look at jars of candy and new books with unbroken bindings and T-shirts that seem funny but we're not sure and gloves that heat up when you rub them together.

Danny is the only one with much money today, and he buys slippers that sing songs when you walk in them and two oversized Tootsie Rolls and a cookbook of chocolate-chip cookie recipes, because I love baking and Danny loves cookies, and if we can't go out together, we at least need to have something wonderful inside.

There's a snow globe in one store, but it's a jokey Florida one, where tiny confetti suns fall when you shake it up, instead of snow. The idea of a snow globe without snow inside makes me so sad I ask if we can sit at the fountain for a minute to recover.

"We need *snow*," I say when we've been sitting in silence for a while. I can't let go of how terrible I think a snowless snow globe is, or how happy Danny looked when he saw the snowy snow globe in the hospital.

Danny nods, solemn.

"I think we really do," he says.

I sneak out my notebook. *Healing power of snow?* I write under the column of hypotheses of things that might help Danny. I smile at the way the words look together—hopeful and easy.

Danny puts on his slippers by the fountain and they sing "Ramblin' Man," which is a song we know because my dad plays it on repeat when he's shaving, and my mother hates it.

My dad says it reminds him of his life as a man on the road.

"Exactly," my mother says. It's the only time I ever really see how badly she wishes he were home all the time.

Danny's cracking up at the slippers and the tinny way the music comes out of them with every step.

Other people stare at him, and it's probably because of the singing slippers, but he also looks skinny and a little pale, even though he's better than he was when I first got to his house.

"We should give these to your dad," he says.

"You know how my mom doesn't think that song's very funny?"

"Sure," Danny says.

"I'm starting to feel like it's not so funny either." My dad's always been gone a lot, and I've never minded too much, but for some reason, the sicker Danny gets, the more I wish my dad were around.

I put on the slippers myself and start stomping my feet in them.

"Lately he's gone so much he doesn't even bother unpacking," I say, and I stomp even harder. Dad brings a big fat duffel bag with him in his truck. But the last couple of months the duffel's been on the floor of the bedroom, clothes spilling out but never quite finding their way back into the drawers.

"He always comes home, though," Danny says.

"Sometimes it feels like his truck is his home. Isn't home wherever you spend the most time?" If we talk too much more, I might cry, and I really don't want to cry. Danny deserves a fun, no-crying day.

"If that's true, the hospital is becoming my home," Danny says, and I think he means it to be a joke, but it's the kind of joke that hurts.

"Someday the mountains will be our home," I say. "We'll be skiers with big knit hats and even bigger sweaters with reindeer and Christmas trees on them. We'll wear boots and mittens. We'll eat fresh snow."

"What do you think snow feels like? Is it fluffy?" Danny asks. We are both fascinated by it. I want to know how it looks and Danny wants to know how it feels, and we both want to sit in it and stick our tongues out and see what happens.

"I hope it's fluffy," I say. "I'll ask my dad."

"I thought maybe we'd see it sometime soon," Danny says. He looks sad, and his forehead is wrinkled with un-Danny-like worry. "Mom and Dad said we could drive north with you maybe. Over Christmas vacation. But I can't go see snow if I can't stay out of the hospital. I'm stuck here."

"Maybe we can go next year. Mom's always saying she'll take us someday. I bet we can convince them to take us next year."

"I'll have to be better by then," Danny says. And I see it: nervousness. He's nervous that he won't be better by next winter. His voices shakes and his knees do a little, too.

Seeing Danny scared scares me.

"You'll be better soon. Look at you now! You feel good right now!" Danny rolls his shoulders and ankles and puts his hand on his forehead like he's checking up on himself. He grins. I think he's still scared underneath the grin, but I love that he can grin anyway.

"You're right! I'm pretty great today. Write down everything we've done. I'm feeling better every minute."

"We're going to figure it out," I say, opening my notebook and scribbling everything I can remember from the forty-five minutes. I take my time looking at Danny. Ms. Mendez says scientists move slowly so that they don't miss anything. His skin has a yellow tinge, but his cheeks are rosy. He isn't coughing or sneezing or holding his stomach like it hurts.

"Promise?" Danny asks. I nod.

"How much money do you have left?" I ask.

"A lot."

Danny and I have never had allowances or anything.

I have a grandmother who sends me forty dollars for my birthday and Christmas, and Danny walks the neighbor's dog sometimes. But lately Danny's been telling me that his parents have been giving him money. I'm not quite used to it, and Mom's face pinches when I talk to her about it.

"They can't afford that," she mumbled to herself the other day when I told her Danny was going to save the money to get us into Disney World. "They have so many bills right now and they're giving Danny their money?" I shrugged. I don't think it was the kind of question she really wanted an answer for anyway.

I try not to hear my mom's voice now when I ask, "Do you think you have enough money for a suitcase?"

Danny eyes me.

"Are we running away?" he asks. We're not, of course. We aren't the running-away type, and I can't run away with my best friend who is mysteriously ill and sometimes turning blue from not breathing or white from not eating.

I love knowing that if I said yes, though, Danny would do it. He'd run away with me.

"It's a someday suitcase," I say. "It's for when we go to the snow. We'll need it someday soon."

"A someday suitcase," Danny says. I think he likes the way it sounds. I do too. "What will we do with it before someday?"

I picture my dad's duffel in the middle of his bedroom—the constant threat of his leaving, the awful feeling it gives me.

"I'll use it in my room," I say. "I can't really explain it, but I don't like having clothes in the closets and my toothbrush in its holder and my socks in a sock drawer if my dad isn't sure where his real home is. I want my own suitcase. If our house isn't Dad's home, I don't want it to be mine either."

It doesn't quite make sense, even to me, but Danny nods like it could make sense, someday. He nods like it doesn't matter if it makes sense or not.

"I'm sorry about your dad," Danny says, and I know he really is. "I'm sure it doesn't feel like home without him."

"I should be used to it," I say. Even though my dad's been on the road forever, I still feel sad about it sometimes. I hate that feelings seem to happen whether or not I want them.

Danny thinks for a great long while. We listen to the fountain spray water, and we listen to the people around us discuss TV sizes and new purses and slurp on their huge sodas. A kid cries. A song we hate plays. A couple starts fighting about something.

"We can be each other's home," Danny says at last.

It's the best thing he's ever said. I can't even speak. When

I'm emotional I lose all my words, but Danny's good at filling in the empty spaces. I get quiet and Danny talks. It's perfect.

It's home.

"All right, we gotta get that suitcase. It's gonna have to be big. Snowsuits seem pretty bulky," Danny says, and the look on his face tells me that he's picturing it—the coats and pants that look more like sleeping bags than clothes, slipping on the ice, lifting his face to the snowfall. "Do you think we'll go sledding?"

"Of course."

So we buy a someday suitcase.

I give ten dollars and Danny gives sixty-five and we get something sleek and purple and it rolls in this precise, floaty way that I like.

"The Someday Suitcase," Danny says, and it sounds like a royal proclamation, a certain future.

~ ~

The next day Danny has a fever so high he goes into the hospital and gets stuck with needles and filled with fluids.

I pack the Someday Suitcase and wait for the Someday.

I beg Mom to let me visit Danny in the hospital instead of going to school on Monday, but she says no and tells me my life can't stop every time Danny gets sick.

"I think it's time to understand that Danny might be sick for a while. For a long while," she says.

I nod.

"Do you have questions?"

I shake my head.

"We should talk about this all," Mom says. "It's a big deal, what's going on with Danny. I want to make sure you understand everything."

"I got it," I say, and Mom makes a face like she knows I'm lying and she's going to have more to say later.

"Dad and I will talk to you more about it anytime you want," Mom says, and just the mention of Dad makes me miss him even more.

⁓

I'm not getting better at being in school without Danny. I keep bumping into his desk and getting bruises on my hips and my knees because he's not there to scoot the desk back and forth when I'm being clumsy. My art projects look sad and unfinished, and I can't remember anything that happens in the book we're reading for class.

I'm starting my walk home when Elsa grabs my arm. I jump. So few people talk to me without Danny around that I almost forget I'm a person in a body.

"Come with us," Elsa says. Her doe eyes are sparkly and her hand is warm. I feel like I'm not supposed to like anyone but Danny, but I like her. And I even like Levi, who is standing to the side and humming something to himself. He reminds me a little of Jake—never doing the same things everyone else is doing, but seeming to enjoy being in his own world. I wonder if they'd get along. I wonder if they'll meet. I wonder if Jake could like Levi as much as he likes Danny.

The thought scares me.

"I should go home . . . ," I say, but I don't really mean it.

"Oh, come on," Elsa says. "Levi's mom's teaching us

yoga and Levi has a trampoline, and his mom almost always has at least five different kinds of ice cream in the freezer."

It sounds pretty good.

⁓

The last time I saw Rachel, it was when she came to class during a unit on families and holidays and traditions and she told us about her favorite Jewish holiday, called Purim, and brought along the best-tasting cookies I'd ever eaten. I've heard she thinks she's psychic or something. She looks younger and cooler than the other moms. She wouldn't let us call her Ms. Goldstein. I've always liked the mysterious gap between her front teeth and the way she tells old stories in a way that makes them interesting.

When we get to Levi's house, she's on the front porch, her body all twisted up like a pretzel.

"Kids!" she says, untangling her limbs and skipping across the lawn to give us all hugs, even me. "I'm so glad to see you, Clover! You have a very warm energy." I blush. She makes it sound like the best thing I could possibly have. Elsa and Levi go inside to get ice cream, and Rachel leans down and whispers to me, "And a little sad too, hmm?"

"Yes," I whisper back. She makes it easy to answer her.

I don't know anything about energy, but I think Levi's mom's energy is perfect—glowy and somehow both calm and exciting at once.

She makes Levi carry a crystal in his backpack and she did tarot card readings at his birthday party last summer. Danny made fun of her for it, and we got into an argument about her.

"I like her," I said. "I like the things she does."

"You like science! This is the opposite of science!" he said.

I couldn't quite explain it at the time, but I know now that science is about believing in *more* things, not less. Science is about possibilities. All of them.

I think Rachel is filled with possibilities.

～✺〜

We don't do yoga.

"It doesn't feel like a yoga moment," Rachel says. Levi rolls his eyes.

"Is it a playing-video-games moment?" he asks. Rachel laughs.

"My boy," she says, which isn't an answer, but Levi takes it to mean that he can go play video games, I guess, leaving me and Elsa with his mom at the kitchen table.

"More ice cream for everyone?" she says, and scoops vanilla and strawberry and raspberry chocolate chip into our bowls. I'm so full I could burst, but I'm not about to stop.

"See?" Elsa says. "Levi's house is the best."

"Danny would love this," I say. I don't think Elsa likes when I bring him up, but I have to make sure everyone knows I'm still thinking about him even though he's not here. "Ice cream is his favorite food."

"How is Danny?" Rachel asks, and I can tell that she knows all about him being sick. It seems like everyone knows. The lifeguard at the pool and the librarian and the postman.

"They don't know exactly what's wrong yet," I say. "But some days he's really okay. I think we'll figure it out." I use the tone of voice the doctors use. I don't want Rachel to be one more person who tells me I'm not going to be able to help. I want her to see that I'm capable of doing more.

"We're praying for him," she says. "It's hard when we don't understand something. But there are a lot of mysteries in the world."

I nod.

"You know why I like all these crystals and yoga poses and energies?" Rachel asks. Elsa has a funny look on her face, like this is a surprise she's been planning for me all along. And I think if I didn't have Danny and she didn't have Levi, Elsa would be my best friend.

"They're fun?" I say. They seem fun—Rachel wears long, noisy earrings and her arms look strong from the yoga. I love the way the crystals look, crowding the counters and mantels. I like the music she plays—people chanting and chimes ringing and long, low notes being held for minutes at a time.

"It can be fun, sure," Rachel says, "but I was sick once too. And when I was sick, I learned about so many different ways that people get better."

"See?!" Elsa says, bouncing in her chair a little.

"No one knew what was wrong with me, but I went to a very special place up north, and they were able to figure it out. And I did a lot of things to get better. Some were things that normal doctors tell you to do—taking pills and having some procedures and getting lots of tests. And a lot of those things helped. And my religious faith helped me too. But we did other things there. Special healing things. The people up north tested everything and tried everything, and you know what? They figured out what was wrong and how to help me get better. So there's always hope, Clover."

I have the crying feeling in my chest. Kindness makes me cry sometimes. Danny says that's silly—kindness makes him smile. But I don't know how to explain it or stop it. It's how I am.

Rachel's like me—she knows that it's better to be open to more possibilities, always.

"I'm trying to keep having hope," I say. "Ms. Mendez says hope and science are very connected. She says science is hope plus facts."

"That's one good science teacher you have," Rachel says.

"See?" Elsa says. "It's going to be okay. You can relax."

"What was the place called?" I ask. "The up-north place that figured you out?"

"The Somerset Clinic," Rachel says, smiling a little, like it's her favorite memory. "It was in Vermont. I spent a very snowy winter there a long, long time ago." I take out my notebook and write down the name. *The Somerset Clinic.* I like the way it sounds. Simple and snowy and a little mysterious. It feels like it could be a place where Danny and I belong. Vermont could definitely be a place we could call home.

I imagine packing up the Someday Suitcase. I imagine rolling it through snowbanks and up mountaintops. I think Danny and me and the Someday Suitcase are about to have an adventure.

I don't say any of that, though.

I do say: "We've always wanted to see the snow." Rachel and Levi and Elsa all know that when I say *we*, I mean me and Danny. I could never mean anyone else.

"It's so beautiful," Rachel says. "And so cold. And so much whiter than I ever thought it would be."

"We should add snow to our weather science fair project," Elsa says. "You sure you don't want to join us, Clover?"

I shake my head. I'd love to study the snow, but I can't do it without Danny. And I don't have any more room in my notebook for lists about other things. It is filling up with endless lists about Danny.

"I have an idea!" Rachel says, and she smiles her little Rachel smile that looks small but feels big. She gets a pile of white construction paper and four pairs of scissors. She calls Levi back into the room and he comes in, bleary eyed and looking a little like a zombie. It's exactly how Jake looks when Mom says he is "video-gamed out."

Rachel folds the construction paper up into a little square and starts cutting funny, random shapes into the edges.

"My mom's weird," Levi says, sighing. "Sorry."

"What's she doing?" Elsa asks. I don't say anything; I just want to watch Rachel be magical.

Rachel doesn't say anything either. She is totally focused on the *snip, snip, snip* of her scissors.

"There," she says at last. "This will either be beautiful or terrible." She shrugs, like either option is fine with her, and I wonder if I could ever be that free. She unfolds the paper and when it's all the way open, I see what it is.

She's made a snowflake.

I grin.

"Can you show us how to do it?" I ask. Rachel grabs even more construction paper.

"We'll make a blizzard for Danny," Elsa says. I'm so relieved she says it, so I don't have to.

Levi is the first one to start cutting, and I'm grateful for that, too.

⁓

We make a blizzard for Danny.

It's the best thing ever—a pile of huge snowflakes, some ugly and some beautiful. They cover the table and the floor, too. They cover the spare seats and our laps. Our fingers get tired from the cutting. We all hold our breath when one gets finished, and exhale when we get to see what kind of snowflake we've made.

They're not cold or wet or falling from the sky, but I think the surprise of each new shape and the wonder of what is being created is a lot like real snow.

I think real snow is shock and wonder and beauty and healing. It is cold and brilliant and clean and special. And our Danny blizzard is all those things too.

I hope so, at least.

14

"Do I look stupid?" Danny asks. "Is it obvious I'm in a wheelchair?"

It's aquarium field trip day a few days later, and Danny surprised me by actually coming, but he has to be in a wheelchair, because he's weak today and his lungs aren't strong enough for a bunch of walking. He wasn't able to come on the bus, so he missed Paloma's imitation of a fish eating pizza and Ms. Mendez handing out a checklist of sea creatures we have to catch sight of during the day. I took an extra one for him.

The doctors decided an outing might be good for Danny, though, and Helen and Ross will do anything the doctors say. "They're zeroing in on an explanation," they keep saying. "They are so close to pinpointing what exactly is going on with our boy." But the sickness he has doesn't have a name yet.

I told Danny's parents about the Somerset Clinic over dinner last night, and they said it didn't sound like a very official place. They said all that travel might make Danny sicker. They said it seemed very expensive and experimental and that our job was to trust the doctors.

Sometimes all adults sound exactly the same, and I wonder if they are all taking some How to Be an Adult class together, where they learn how to say frustrating things and how to stop listening while pretending to keep listening.

"You don't look stupid," I say. I try to be a little like Mom—direct and honest, even though it might not be what Danny wants to hear. "But I think everyone will know you're in a wheelchair. It's sort of hard to hide."

Danny grimaces.

"I can walk fine," he says.

"I know."

"I can probably walk better than you. You walk so slow."

"You're right." Right now Danny looks so sick that I want to agree with everything he says, just to try to make him feel better.

"Maybe I shouldn't go," he says. Danny's never scared,

but lately he's always scared, and that means the whole world feels off-kilter. Ms. Mendez says we are all part of a huge ecosystem and that there's a balance. She says that's why we have to worry about the environment. "The world is really amazing. It's all very delicate and balanced, and when we hurt one part of the world—the atmosphere, the animals, the trees—it hurts all the other parts. It throws off the balance."

I think I understand about the ecosystem and the special balance of the world now more than ever. Danny and I are part of the ecosystem too, and if something changes between us, everything starts to fall apart.

Danny's in a wheelchair. He's coughing, and we don't know what's wrong with him, and worst of all, he's scared. We have upset the balance of the universe and the special ecosystem of our friendship, and that is very dangerous indeed.

"You're coming to the aquarium," I say. "I want to see all the symbiosis."

"And all the fish," Danny says with a smile that says some things are the same. I am serious and Danny is goofy and together we are absolutely perfect.

⁓

Everyone is happy to see Danny at the aquarium.

"Are you coming back to school?" Marco asks. He gets

too close, and normally Danny would take a big step back to get some space, but in the wheelchair it's a little harder, so he mostly scrunches his face and looks over his shoulder.

"No," Helen answers for him. "Not anytime soon."

My heart squeezes. That wasn't the right answer.

"Danny! Can I take a ride in your wheelchair?" Paloma asks. Danny squirms.

"No, he has to stay in the chair," Helen answers for him again.

"What's wrong with you anyway?" Brandy asks. She has a pursed mouth and always asks questions that sound mean, even though I don't think she wants them to sound mean.

"I'm sick," Danny says, finally answering for himself. "I'm really, really sick."

He coughs again, but the cough isn't quite so bad as it was a few minutes ago. It sounds a little more like a normal cough and a little less like a broken garbage disposal.

When the cough is over, he smiles a little.

"My throat's all cleared up," he says. "I think my cough is gone."

"That's not how coughs work," Helen says, but I know Danny's right. He can get better. He *can*.

⁓⁓

Ms. Mendez has a clipboard and a big smile. "There's a lot to see," she says. "But today we're focusing on symbiosis, okay? Who remembers what that is?"

We should all remember what that is. We've been talking about it since the day Danny got sick, which was approximately a trillion years ago.

Still, only a few of us raise our hands. I guess a lot of people forget to pay attention in science class. It's too bad for them. They are missing out on so many beautiful science-y things.

I raise my hand higher than everyone else and wave it a little bit. I bounce up and down on my toes.

"Clover, why don't you remind us all?" Ms. Mendez says. I think she picks me because she knows how much it means to me. Ms. Mendez is the best teacher in the world.

"Symbiosis is when two organisms help each other and survive together. They each do something special for the other one, and they basically keep each other alive by helping in these funny little ways." I take a deep breath. I'm getting excited just thinking about it.

"That's exactly right," Ms. Mendez says. "And today we're going to see symbiosis in action, and maybe it will inspire us to think about symbiosis in our own lives."

"Maybe!" Brandy says, because she likes to get the last word in, even when she wasn't really involved with the conversation in the first place.

Danny doesn't say anything.

"Off we go!" Ms. Mendez says.

We walk past colorful creatures that I wish I could stare at all day and floating algae and schools of the tiniest fish I've ever seen.

I'm in charge of Danny's wheelchair. He begged Helen not to walk around with us.

"Clover's got it!" he said.

"I don't want to make Clover do all that work."

"Oh, I don't mind! It will be fun!" I said, and we both made puppy-dog eyes and fluttered our eyelashes. Helen eventually agreed that she would sit in the lobby but we had to run and get her if Danny's cough started up again or if he complained about feeling faint or his stomach was acting up.

"Just because he's okay right this second doesn't mean he's not sick," Helen said to me. She had a serious look on her face, and I wished I could unhear her words.

In the first long hallway we catch sight of starfish, and Ms. Mendez promises us we can go by later and touch one.

"There's a whole interactive pool," she says. "We'll get our hands wet, pet a few different sea creatures. How's that sound?"

There's a clamoring of excitement.

"Not yet, though," she says, trying to quiet everyone down. "Not quite yet. First: eels and shrimp!"

The aquarium focuses on animals interacting naturally with their environments instead of just being pretty or identifiable. We get to see something *happen*.

When we get to the electric eels, even Marco and Brandy are quiet. The eels look like snakes, but with a neon tint and this perfect way of moving around the water. Everyone else seems to like dolphins or sea horses best, but now that I'm here, I think maybe I actually am in love with electric eels most of all. They look like they're part of the water, not simply swimming through it. And when Ms. Mendez explains that they're able to deliver big electric shocks, I get a shiver along my spine. Being near them at all gives me a little shock, to be honest.

"Yes," I say under my breath. I step close to the glass and try not to blink as they pass by.

"They're okay," Danny says. "Do you think we'll see any sharks?"

"These are better than sharks!"

"No way. Dolphins are the best. Then sharks," he says. I notice he isn't coughing at all and he's actually arguing with me, which means he's got more energy than usual. I look at his face. It's downright rosy.

"You're fighting with me!" I say, and he gets it. He grins and nods and scoots forward in his wheelchair, like he's about ready to pop himself out.

"I feel kind of great," he says.

"I bet it's the eel," I say, smiling.

"I don't know what it is, but I'll take it." Danny watches the eel too, not as bored as he usually is by science class. "Yeah," he says at last, like he really had to give it a lot of thought. "They're pretty good, I guess."

"Here comes one," Ms. Mendez says. "I want you to look at his mouth."

All twenty of us step toward the glass, our breath fogging it up a little. I want everyone to be quiet and still so I can focus.

"What do you see?" Ms. Mendez asks.

"The snake's eating a gross bug!" Cornell says.

"It's not a snake, it's an eel," I say.

"And that's not a bug in his mouth. There aren't bugs in the water," Gloria says. She rolls her eyes at Cornell. Gloria is the second best in science, after me. "I think the thing in his mouth is a shrimp."

"That's right, Gloria!" Ms. Mendez says, getting more excited by the minute. That's one more thing I love about Ms. Mendez. Sometimes she gets so excited I think she might explode in front of us. Ms. Fitch is the same way. When she's excited, it shows. She was even excited about our going to the aquarium. In art class next week, we're going to focus on drawing and painting and sculpting the fish we saw today.

I smile because even when some things are hard and

sad, the world is always full of fish and science and art.

"That's gross," Brandy says, turning away from the eel.

"Not gross!" Ms. Mendez says. "Because guess what? That eel isn't actually eating the shrimp!"

"Yes, it is," Danny says. He's even arguing with Ms. Mendez now, a really great sign. I squeeze the handle of his wheelchair. I take out my notebook and make some notes about how Danny's doing. *Cheeks like strawberry frozen yogurt,* I write. *Little coughing. Good energy.*

"I promise you it's not, Danny," Ms. Mendez says. "Look closely." We all try to look closer. If we could, we'd jump right in that pool, I think. "The shrimp is cleaning the eel's teeth! And in return, the shrimp is finding some food to eat in there."

"That is disgusting," Brandy says.

"Ew, that's so cool!" Cornell says.

"That's symbiosis," Gloria says.

"That is exactly right," Ms. Mendez says. "How amazing is that! The shrimp is getting food, and in exchange the eel gets a nice clean mouth, and they exist together like that, helping each other along the way. It's pretty magnificent, really."

I think Ms. Mendez might cry from how much she likes symbiosis, but instead she brings us around to see symbiosis with crabs and anemones and clown fish and angelfish and

gobies and more shrimp, all with special symbiotic relationships.

Sometime around the clown fish, Danny stands up out
of his wheelchair. I would worry, but he looks so strong
I don't even think about it. Ms. Mendez asks us to take a
break and draw our favorite fish so that we'll have something to work from in art class next week, and Danny lets
me sit in his chair to do mine.

Instead of drawing fish, though, I try to take in every
single thing around us to figure out why Danny is feeling so
much better. It's like he's not even sick.

Maybe he's *not* sick! Maybe he just needs fish around
him! I write that down in my hypothesis column and pon-
der whether that's possible.

I'm pretty sure it's not.

I try to think about what else is different today. Maybe
the temperature of the aquarium—very cold from air-
conditioning—helps his lungs somehow? Maybe he needs
to be in a wheelchair for a little while every day, to give his
lungs a rest? Maybe the treatments they tried at the hospital
last week are finally working, and it just took a little more
time than they thought it would? None of those solutions
feels right, so I keep trying to stretch my mind every which
way to figure out what it could be that's making Danny feel
better today.

I look back over my old notes to look at other times Danny was doing well. I'm looking for a common denominator.

I flip back and forth between the pages.

I'm starting to see something.

I flip some more.

I look at Danny again. He's laughing with Marco like a maniac. He's laughing so hard it would normally make him bend over in a fit of coughing. He's laughing so hard he looks exactly the way he always used to: vibrant and silly and raucous and healthy.

I think I see the common denominator.

I think I have a new hypothesis for how to make Danny feel better.

It's me.

When I'm around, Danny gets better.

I look at the eel and the shrimp in its mouth and the way the two creatures exist perfectly together.

"What happens if the eel doesn't have the shrimp, or the shrimp doesn't have the eel?" I ask, forgetting to raise my hand. Ms. Mendez doesn't seem to mind.

"That can't happen, Clover," she says. "They need each other to survive."

"Right," I say, because I already knew that. "Symbiosis."

I look at Danny and think the word again in my head.

Symbiosis. When you need each other to survive.

The class starts to move on, but I stare at the way the eel never clamps down on the shrimp's little body, the way the shrimp is fearless in the eel's terrifying mouth.

I get it.

15

That night Jake decides he's no longer eating any food that isn't white.

"Rice," he says, when Mom tries to give him spinach.

"Yogurt," he says, when Mom tries to give him an orange.

"Mashed potatoes," he says, when Mom tries to give him asparagus.

And when Mom brings out the pasta with meat sauce—her specialty—Jake grabs a spoon and starts scooping the sauce off the pasta and dropping it on the center of the table.

It's one of Jake's tantrums, and it's a bad one, a messy one. With Dad back on the road, Mom and I have to take care of it together, and Mom's out of sorts today. I think she's missing Dad as much as I am. We all are, I guess.

Jake uses his hands to strip even more of the sauce from the noodles, and Mom turns red and I think she might cry. Her eyes go glassy and she keeps her mouth shut really tight like she doesn't want anything to escape.

If it were me throwing a fit, I'd have to clean up, but Jake is in no shape to be told to do anything at all, so Mom takes charge. While Mom sponges and paper-towels and mumbles under her breath, I calm Jake down.

"There's plain pasta left in the pot," I say, and I get him a bowl with some butter, which is almost white. "But you can't eat only white food every day. Let's have a red day tomorrow and eat tomatoes and strawberries. And a yellow lemonade and banana day the day after that."

"But then we have to have an all-green day," Jake says. Jake and I agree about green vegetables—we do not like them, even though we know they are good for us and Mom does a celebratory dance when we eat them.

"Yes," I say, using my dramatic-sad voice that Jake loves. "We will have to have a green day. It will be tragic. But after that we will do a BROWN day and eat chocolate and burgers for every meal!"

"BROWN FOOD DAY!" Jake yelps, his hands in the air, cheering us on.

"BROWN FOOD DAY!" I call back, because I know Jake loves it when I repeat whatever he's doing. He then likes to repeat me, and we can go in circles like that forever. It's annoying for me and Mom, but it makes Jake so happy that it ends up making us happy too.

Mom smiles at me and mouths *thank you*.

I think we are a little symbiotic family. It's not perfect symbiosis—I think Mom has to work hardest of all, and Dad being gone makes the whole equation a little crooked sometimes, but we all work together and give things up and make things work so that everyone can survive.

Mom sits back down and the table's clean and she doesn't even yell at Jake, and for once it doesn't make me mad—it's okay that Jake can get away with some things that I can't get away with. We're different. We have different roles in our symbiotic family.

"Tell me about the aquarium today," Mom says while she and I start eating our pasta, meat sauce still intact.

"It was perfect. Especially because Danny came. He made everything even better."

Mom looks up at the ceiling and at Jake slurping on his noodles and at her own plate of spaghetti. She brings her whole mostly uneaten meal to the kitchen.

I hear her sniffle.

I think for a second maybe she's still upset about Jake's

tantrum, but that's not it. We all were just fine about that a few minutes ago. We fixed it.

"Jake, can you play in your room?" she says before we're actually done eating.

"Yes," Jake says. And for as many strange and impossible rules as Jake has, he also will sometimes be so easy and clear and no-nonsense. He can play just fine in his room, so he will.

Once he's gone, I start helping with the dishes. I wonder if I should try again to explain about Danny. There's still this well of misunderstanding in the room with us.

"You don't always have to help, Clover," Mom says. I'm confused, because she's always, always bugging me about helping with the dishes and the trash and the dirty bathroom.

"Yes, I do," I say, and gather up the glasses.

"You don't have to always help everyone else. You can just take care of you."

I look at her like she's an alien speaking pig Latin.

"Are you talking about the dishes?"

"I'm talking about the dishes and Jake. But mostly I'm talking about Danny."

When she says his name, it sounds like an accusation. I almost drop the glasses.

"Never mind. I don't want to talk any more about

Danny," I say, even though if I'm honest, all I want to do is talk about Danny—how I figured everything out at the aquarium, how to make him better, how to get to Vermont.

"You need to get used to doing things without him," Mom says. She says it all in one breath, like a gust of wind. And I know from the way it swooshed out of her that she didn't really want to say it but felt like she had to.

It doesn't help.

It doesn't make me less mad at her.

It doesn't make me less scared.

I want to throw a Jake-style tantrum in her direction, hearing those words.

I think I could, too. I feel a push and pull and burn and chill inside me all at once.

"I'll never get used to doing things without Danny," I say, as calm as I possibly can, which isn't very calm at all.

"He's very sick, Clover," Mom says in a whisper. She clears her throat, shakes her head, pulls back her shoulders, and tries again. She wants me to know she means it. "Danny is very, very sick. And when someone's sick and we can't figure out why, some things change. I'm not saying this to hurt you. I'm saying this because I want you to be prepared."

"For what?"

The table is cleared, but I sort of keep wandering between the kitchen and the dining room anyway, traveling the same path even though there's nothing at all for me to carry.

"I want you to be prepared for the possibility that Danny won't be around as much. I want you to even try to be prepared for the possibility that Danny . . . that he won't get better."

She says it plain and simple. It's not meant to be cruel, but it is.

Mom is saying impossible things in our dirty kitchen, and I'm not sure I'm going to be able to keep down my pasta.

She's always talked to me this way. I remember when she first told me about Jake.

"Jake has a type of autism, and that's going to be challenging sometimes." I nodded. "I know that it's easier if you and Jake have all the same rules and all the same punishments and if everything's nice and even and fair. But that's not how it's going to be, because Jake's going to need different things than you. You're going to be mad about it sometimes, and that's just fine. If you're mad, you come tell me and Dad so you don't take it out on Jake. But we're going to ask you be to understanding even when he sometimes won't understand."

Back then, I liked the way Mom said things in nice clear words. I liked that she'd answer all the questions honestly, even when she knew I wouldn't like the answers. I liked that she never pretended things were going to be easier than they were. It meant that on all the really great days with Jake, I could feel happy, and on the hard days I didn't feel so disappointed.

But right now, I hate the clean, crisp words Mom's using. They're icy and awful.

"You're wrong," I say. I try to sound just as sure and clear and direct as she did. "I have a solution. We need to get to the Somerset Clinic in Vermont. And once we get to Vermont, everything will be fine. In Vermont they can tell Danny what is wrong, and they'll find out how to fix it and everything will go back to exactly the way it's always been."

"Vermont?" Mom says. She has a sad look on her face, and I know it's because she thinks I don't understand, but it's definitely Mom who doesn't understand.

"The Somerset Clinic," I say, making sure she hears every word and how beautiful it sounds. "It's in Vermont, and I looked it up online and it's perfect. Levi's mom, Rachel, told me about it. It's going to fix everything."

Mom's forehead wrinkles and her head cocks to the side.

"I don't know what that is, honey."

"I keep trying to tell you! And stop calling me *honey!*" I say, louder than I intended.

"Okay. Deep breaths," Mom says. "Let's take some nice deep breaths."

Jake appears at the door to the kitchen. He doesn't like yelling unless he's the one doing it. Usually I would never yell when Jake's around, but right now I'm unstoppable. I'm going to yell. I'm going to yell *loud*.

"You're not listening! You need to help us get to Vermont! If we can get to Vermont, everything will be fine!"

Mom doesn't reply.

I don't know if she doesn't believe me or doesn't believe in the clinic or maybe just hates Vermont. But I do know that she's already decided not to help.

"Danny's parents are doing absolutely everything they can," she says. "You have to trust that."

But I don't trust that. If they were doing everything they could, Danny would be in Vermont and not spending so much time in stupid hospital beds eating Jell-O and rubbery chicken and iceberg lettuce.

That's when I know it for absolutely sure, even though I mostly knew it already: it's up to me to get Danny better.

List of Cures Danny's Doctors Have Tried

- Antibiotics
- Two hospital stays
- IVs full of things to make his blood better
- Antihistamines
- Steroids
- Injections that Danny says don't hurt but I think must hurt
- Going to other doctors and seeing if they can fix him
- A wheelchair

16

The sound of Danny not breathing is awful and wakes me up in the middle of the night when I sleep over on Friday night. I haven't told him my symbiosis hypothesis yet. I think it needs further testing, so I begged and pleaded to spend the night at Danny's, even though Mom thinks I should be trying to "get a little distance."

I promised her I'd invite Elsa over for a sleepover next weekend. She sighed and said okay and kissed my forehead to let me know it really was okay and she's on my side, even when it seems like she's not.

Danny and I helped Ross make pizzas and after we researched more about Vermont and the Somerset Clinic, and I convinced him to show me pictures of the grandfather who was once sick like Danny. He didn't let me ask his parents all about the grandfather, so there are still gaps in my research, of course.

Ms. Mendez says an ideal experiment doesn't have any gaps, but almost no experiments are ideal.

I'm not thinking of Ms. Mendez now, though. The sounds Danny's making are so terrible they push all the dreams and thoughts and wonderings right out of my brain. There's only room for fear.

It's a sputtering, trying-too-hard noise. He's in the room next door because Helen thought if we stayed in the same room Danny might not get his rest. Listening to Danny is like listening to a storm right on the other side of the wall, so I grab my notebook from under my pillow and rush to him before anyone else wakes up and gets there.

Even worse than the sound of his tortured breathing is the color of his face—a terrible almost-purple that looks even scarier in the orange light of his nightlight (the one he made me promise to never tell anyone about). The new shade makes me freeze in the doorway. I'm not sure I can be in the same space as someone with purple skin, someone making awful wheezing sounds. For an instant, I forget he's Danny at all. He's only a person I want to get away from.

Then I tell myself, *That's your best friend. Do something,* and my body finally listens to my mind and I run to his side.

Danny splits in the middle, his head and neck and torso rocking toward his knees, like that might help the cough come out more easily. I guess I'm getting here just in time.

I tell the fear in me to quiet down and I put my hand on his back and wonder if he's choking on something in particular or nothing at all. I like explanations, but with Danny it's so hard to find them. I hear Ms. Mendez in my head, telling me explanations are there, whether I have them yet or not.

It calms me down. A little. I focus on the science and research and my method. I am testing to see if my symbiosis theory is right. Maybe I can be the one who fixes Danny.

I think I should also make a special section in my research notebook about other people who have had weird symptoms for no reason. Historical context, Ms. Mendez called it. Precedent. I have so much more work to do, if I want to do this well. When we get to the clinic, I think I'll meet a lot of people with mysterious illnesses, and if I can learn about them, it will help me learn about Danny.

I wish we were at the clinic right now, getting answers, instead of here in Danny's bedroom, getting more questions.

Jake likes me to rub his back at night sometimes too. It calms him down when he's having nightmares or tantrums or a hard time sleeping. I wish I were good at more things than back rubbing and knowing what Danny and Jake need, but at least there's a cricket buzz outside the window and the perfect slant of moonlight coming through.

Maybe this is who I'm meant to be—a person who makes other people feel better.

In the ecosystem, every creature has a role, and I think this might be mine. It makes me a little sad—I wish my role were something more exciting, like discovering a second moon or saving whales from extinction, but I try to remember that every single role in the ecosystem matters, even if the job is small and silly-seeming.

I bet the shrimp in the eel's mouth doesn't think it has the most exciting job, either.

Danny's breath gets clearer, crisper. It starts to sound less like a grumbling monster and more like a person.

His face returns to a color that isn't that terrible purple, and the wildness that's in his eyes whenever the illness reaches some terrifying height is gone too. He's Danny again.

"You saved me," he says.

"Did you swallow something? Were you eating in bed? Was there something in your throat? Are you allergic to something?" I ask. I still want reasons, even if I know they're not always there.

"I couldn't breathe," Danny says. There's a crease in his forehead where wonder lives. It deepens when we see bright rainbows from our lawns or elephants at the zoo. He is full of it now, the wonder, but I can't imagine why. I'm the only thing he can see.

"That was like magic," Danny says.

My palms are wet and my heart is loud.

I write *magic?* in the margin of my notebook, and I know it's the moment I'm supposed to tell Danny what I realized at the aquarium, what I think I just proved right this second, that our symbiosis is so much bigger than the statue game and the fact that I like pizza crusts and he likes pizza toppings. But I'm not ready. I need more time to be regular Clover before I become Possibly Lifesaving Clover.

"You're okay," I say, instead of telling him all the things I should be telling him. "You're going to be okay. We'll tell the people in the clinic all about your cough."

Danny puts his hand on his chest and his mouth turns down. He's tearing up. It's probably because things seem sadder at night than they do during the day. But still, Danny doesn't usually cry.

"We need to get there soon," he says, and I think about what Mom said the other day—that Danny might not get better. I take his temperature and wish I could look at his X-rays and his bloodwork and his grandfather's medical records and make sense of it all. I wish I knew more about symbiosis and immunodeficiencies, which is a word I have heard Helen and Ross mutter, and it took me three times to write it down correctly. I wish I knew how lungs work and what things someone needs in their blood to make their blood perfect.

"I'm glad you're here," Danny says when he's drifting back off to sleep.

"I'm glad I'm here too," I say, meaning something entirely different.

I flip though the notebook in my lap while Danny starts to snore. I know about correlation and causation from Ms. Mendez. Just because Danny feels better when I'm around doesn't mean I'm making him better. For a hypothesis to be good, it has to show causation. Maybe there is no causation. Maybe my hypothesis is all kinds of wrong. Maybe this is all random, a faulty experiment. Danny and I spend a lot of time together, so statistically speaking it would make sense that his good days are with me. He's had bad days with me too. When he first fainted, I was right next to him.

I lean to his chest. His heart is powerful. His breathing is clear. His skin is rosy and sweet-smelling, a fact I'm a little embarrassed to know. I rest my hand on his forehead. It's cool and dry and exactly like mine.

"Good scientists follow their instincts," Ms. Mendez

says, and I know what my instincts say.

I am saving Danny.

But now that Danny feels better, I'm the one who's unsteady.

I think it might be happening. The thing Ms. Mendez talked about. The unexpected; the unlikely; the startling.

17

We sit on opposite sides of the table and pick at what we call the Menagerie of Awful, which is a collection of everything the food court has to offer: plasticky pizza, Chinese food so salty the taste makes us groan and stick our tongues out, McDonald's fries, chicken fingers, cinnamon-sugar pretzels, an enormous vanilla milk shake, and a bacon-bacon-bacon burger with a side of guacamole. These are the only foods Danny claims aren't upsetting his stomach today.

Helen and Ross never found out about Danny's coughing fit last night or the way he soaked through his sheets with sweat before I showed up. That's the only reason they've let us come to the mall.

"This tastes awesome," Danny says, licking ketchup off his hand and moaning at the goodness of milk shakes. "I think it's finally over. I think I got better all on my own. I was scared for a second there, Clo. I didn't want to tell you, but I really was scared."

I have to tell him.

I push fries and chicken fingers closer to him. I think he'll need fries and chicken fingers for this.

"I found a pattern," I say. "I found what helps you feel better."

"I *am* better," Danny says. "You don't need to do research on me anymore, because I'm not sick anymore. My cough went away and my throat doesn't hurt, and my ears and nose are all clear and my stomach doesn't ache, and I bet if they took blood again, they'd see that there's nothing to worry about. I can tell. I'm better."

"I don't think you're better," I say, and my heart breaks to have to make his smile disappear. "I think you just *feel* better."

"Isn't that the same thing?" Danny asks, but he knows it isn't. He sighs. He fidgets. He eats more fries. "Is it hamburgers?" he asks. "Because this burger is awesome, and I'm really sick of all the spinach Mom is making me eat."

"Why would it be hamburgers?" I ask.

Danny shrugs. "I don't know. I feel great right now and I'm eating a burger. Or maybe it's playing video games? That'd be cool! Then I'd have to stop going to school and play video games all the time!"

Danny has trouble focusing sometimes.

"But you miss school," I say.

"That's true. Maybe it's swimming? Is it swimming? I think I feel pretty good when we're at the pool, right?" He is all lit up. He's practically bouncing off the walls, thinking of all the wonderful things he'll be able to do if his illness is cured by hamburgers and video games and the water. "If it's water, we can go to water parks every day!" he says. He's in his own Danny-world now. He's talking so fast it's hard to keep up. "It will be mandatory, going on water slides! How cool will that be?"

"Danny," I say, but he's still thinking about water parks. "*Danny*. It's not water or food or anything like that."

His face drops.

I take a big breath. The biggest one ever.

"It's me," I say.

Danny doesn't say anything at first. He crinkles his forehead and looks at me hard, like I might be lying.

"It's you being close to me," I say. "When I'm around, you feel better."

My notebook is on the table with our Menagerie of

Awful, and Danny grabs it and starts looking through it. He squints at some of the pages. I'm worried about how he's taking all of this, but I'm also pretty proud of the neat way my research looks on the page. I highlighted relevant information. I didn't scribble or doodle or use my messy handwriting. I did a really good job.

Danny chews his lips and flips pages.

"It's you," he says, testing out the words.

"It's a hypothesis," I say. I'm hoping Danny paid enough attention in science class to remember that a hypothesis is an unproven but possible thing.

Danny leans closer to me. I'm not sure if it's on purpose or by accident, but I can tell he already believes me. "That's why I feel so good today."

"I don't know why or how or anything else, but if you look at the research—"

"Stop talking like a scientist, Clo," Danny says. "Talk like my friend."

"Remember the fish? The symbiosis? I think we're like that."

"We're like fish."

"Kind of," I say. "I don't know. Think of the way we fit together. The statue game. That you're silly when I'm shy and that I'm organized when you're spacey."

"Yeah . . ."

"Don't tell your parents."

"Why not? They'll be so happy."

I can't say why not, exactly. But I'm sure I don't want anyone else to know.

"We need to focus on getting you to the Somerset Clinic," I say. "That's the most important thing."

"To see snow," Danny says.

"And to figure out what's wrong," I say.

"Does it matter what's wrong if it's all okay when you're here?" he says. I can see his mind working, and I don't like the direction it's going. I don't want to be responsible. Not even for my very best friend in the entire world.

I don't know how to answer.

"I can't be here all the time," I say, and as soon as I say it I know I shouldn't have.

"Oh," Danny says. He looks down. He stops eating.

Danny never stops eating when there's the Menagerie of Awful in front of him.

"You know what I mean. I want you to be better forever. Good scientists get answers. Good scientists ask for help."

"I understand," Danny says, but I don't think he does.

"Plus, don't you want to go to Vermont? It's our chance. It's *snow*, Danny."

His feelings are still hurt, I can see it all over his face, but snow is our special thing, so he finally looks up from his lap.

"It gets stuck in your eyelashes," he says. "The snow. It gets stuck in your eyelashes and you can eat it. And footprints. I want to make footprints in the snow."

I want that too. I want to run through it. I want snow boots that leave holes in the snow where my feet were. I want there to be a clear path of where I'm going and where I've been.

"We'll get there," I say.

"We have to," Danny says, and finally we're on the same page again.

We decide without words to stop talking about his sickness. We will do the things we are best at, the things that make us Danny and Clover. We order a second round of burgers and an extra order of scallion pancakes and a tub of soy sauce for dipping. Later, we will come up with the world's best plan for getting to Vermont.

"What's your favorite thing about the mall?" Danny says. I've missed his questions, the ones he already knows the answers to.

"You," I say.

Danny blushes.

We aren't usually sweet with each other. It's not part of our special brand of symbiosis. He squirms and I squirm too, and I'm about to apologize for saying something cheesy when Elsa's voice breaks through our conversation. I hear her laugh and Levi's snort—they are unmistakable, wonderful sounds.

The sounds give my heart a happy leap, then a guilty twinge.

I shouldn't want to turn around to see the faces of my new friends. But I do. I really, really do.

And there they are: at the other end of the food court, Elsa and Levi are laughing and wearing sneakers and being cool. When I see them, I wonder what they're talking about and if they'll tell me later and when we can hang out next.

Then I stop myself from thinking that. If I am the person who is going to fix Danny, I don't have time for other friends.

But.

But.

Elsa has a bracelet that shines in the ugly mall lighting and Levi is saying something about his mom and her newest book of Zen meditations. There's an empty chair across the table from them that looks almost like it's meant for me.

It's hard to squash down some feelings, once they start to push their way up.

"Elsa and Levi are eating Chinese food over there," I say, even though I know I should stay quiet. Danny and I only need each other.

Ms. Mendez says symbiosis is simple. I try to make my brain focus on the simplicity. Danny plus Clover equals Everything I Need.

"Elsa and Levi are here?" Danny asks. He gets a funny smile on his face, like he's hiding something very un-smile-like underneath it. I know his faces well, and this is a bad-news face.

On top of recently being in charge of cataloging Danny's illness, I'm also keeping a list in my head of everything his face does. His face, it turns out, does a lot. Over the course of an hour it takes a hundred different shapes. Some people have happy and sad and asleep and that's about it. I think I'm like that. Danny has all these mini feelings, in-between expressions. The way leaves in places like Vermont change from green to yellow to orange to red to brown over the course of the year, with all sorts of shades along the way.

Danny has hundreds of seasons. He is nothing like Florida, which is maybe part of why I love him so much.

The season on his face now is like the beginning of spring somewhere in Not Florida. Trying to be warm, but still too chilly for a walk without a jacket, still determined to surprise you with rain.

"Elsa has big ears," Danny says. "And Levi doesn't know how to read out loud. Have you ever noticed that? He stumbles over every word."

Danny is never mean, but he's being a little mean.

"You're being too loud," I say, since I don't want to tell him he's mean.

Neither of us is supposed to be mean to anyone.

"Maybe that's today's symptom," Danny says. He smiles even bigger. The thing underneath it grows, too. "Volume control." He says it so loudly I know it's not an accident at all.

"I thought today's symptom was being cold," I say since Danny's in a red sweater and thick socks. Elsa has on a shirt that is my favorite shade of purple, and Levi is using chopsticks to pick up rice. I watch their mouths and try to decipher what's making them laugh so hard.

"The illness is mysterious," Danny says. "You know that. Volume control could BE A THING." He is pleased with himself, yelling that last part. We're sitting in the perfect part of the food court for his voice to echo.

"We should go say hi. We could hang out with them for a little." I say it knowing I shouldn't.

"Why?" Danny slurps the end of the milk shake without asking if I want some more. "You see them all the time at school. Seeing me is obviously more important. You said so yourself. You have to stay near me to help me."

"Wasn't it nice the other day? To be around everyone again?"

Danny shrugs. "What's your favorite food in the

Menagerie of Awful?" he asks. He won't even look in Elsa and Levi's direction.

"They're going to get up in a minute—let's go over."

Ms. Mendez says scientists use both their heads and their hearts, but she doesn't say what to do when your head and your heart disagree.

"You love answering my questions," Danny says. "Why won't you answer my question?"

I look at the remnants of all the terrible food we just ate. "Egg rolls," I say. "Ones that were obviously frozen about ten minutes ago and need to be drowned in soy sauce."

"You used to like desserts best." Danny polishes off the french fries and the pepperoni from the pizza, like he's supposed to.

"Things change," I say, and I mean it to be light, like an elbow nudge of a sentence, but it hits him hard.

Danny has a steamy summer rainstorm look on his face—like it was nice out but I've ruined it.

Elsa gets up to bring her tray to the trash cans and sees me. There's a moment where it looks like she's choosing whether or not to say hi, and it takes me waving to snap her out of it.

"I'm cold again," Danny says. "I need to buy another scarf." I know that means he probably has a fever, but I pretend not to hear him.

"Hey, Elsa!" I call out.

"Clover! And Danny! You're out and about again! That's awesome! Are you coming back to school for good this week?"

"Maybe." Danny looks at the table like he's going to eat even more, but there's not really much of anything there.

Right away I feel bad. He doesn't want to explain. He doesn't want to tell them the aquarium might have been a one-time thing. He doesn't really want to answer any questions. And I should know that. Because Danny asks questions and I answer them, and that's how it's supposed to be.

"Danny doesn't have to go anymore," I say, trying so hard to do the right thing even though I can't figure out what the right thing is. I try to make it sound cool and fun—that Danny is above school. That he doesn't need it anymore.

Elsa tries to find more to say. "It's—you're—do you have to do homework or are you too sick, or I mean tired, to do that kind of—I mean—does Clover tell you what we're doing in all the different—"

"Clover tells me everything," Danny says.

Elsa doesn't know what to say to that and neither do I.

"Hey, guys," Levi says when he makes his way over. He doesn't know what to say either. "At the mall, huh?"

"You guys buying stuff?" I ask. My voice is too high for normal conversation. Dogs could hear it.

"My mom's making me get dressed up for my brother's bar mitzvah," Levi says. "So I'm sort of looking for a tie and a nice shirt, but mostly we're wandering."

"Shopping for ties is way boring," Elsa says. "I thought it might be like shopping for clothes. But it's not. Everything's striped."

"Not everything," Levi says. He looks at the ceiling, reconsidering. "Almost everything."

There is a space in the conversation where they are supposed to ask if we want to wander with them, but nothing fills that space. It stays empty and awkward, and Danny scratches his nose and shivers.

"Are you okay?" I ask, trying to fix all the mistakes I'm making, trying to be a better best friend.

"I gotta get out of the cold," Danny says. "Maybe buy a scarf." Levi laughs and Elsa laughs, and they both have to stop when they realize that Danny's not laughing.

"Scarves are cool!" Elsa says with too much enthusiasm. "Clover should get one too, for Vermont."

I startle. Danny wouldn't like that I told Elsa and Levi about the Somerset Clinic, even though I only found out through them. He wouldn't like that they know anything at all about our big plans and our love of snow and how

165

desperately we are trying to figure out what's wrong with him.

I don't think Danny wants them to know anything about him at all.

"Scarves are totally cool," Levi says. "Kinda like ties, actually. So, yeah. Same thing."

I want to become a table or a piece of discarded pizza crust. I hope that Danny will say something light and airy, the way he used to, the way he's supposed to do. I hope that Danny will see how kind Elsa is and how gentle Levi is and maybe even invite them into our world a little.

Sometimes I hope for things that will never, ever happen.

Sometimes I can't help but hope for impossible things.

It isn't very scientific of me at all.

"No," Danny says, "scarves aren't like ties at all."

He storms off with all our trays of food piled on top of each other, and I silently beg him not to drop them before he gets to the garbage cans. When something is already terrible, I am scared of it getting worse.

With Danny lately, things are always getting worse.

I have solved one part of the Danny Experiment, but there are bigger questions now, about how to be a good friend and also myself. I don't think I understand who needs what, and if there is room enough for my needs too. I want to ask someone what it means that I can save him, and why it doesn't feel good to be saving him.

"You're so nice to him," Elsa says.

I'm supposed to answer that Danny's my best friend, so I'm not being nice, I'm being his friend. I should answer that Danny and I are so close we're practically the same, so if Danny's sick, I'm sick.

I don't say any of those things.

～✺

"You told them about Vermont?" Danny says on our way out of the mall a few minutes later. He is stormy and chilly.

"They told me about Vermont," I say. "Levi's mom did."

"Vermont is ours," Danny says.

"I know."

"They're not invited," Danny says.

"I *know*."

I think I'm going to cry.

"All I need is you and me and the snow," Danny says.

"I know," I say. I wonder at the way he looks healthy and strong after a few hours with me.

And it scares me, but it also is the most joyful thing in the world, to see Danny the way he's supposed to be.

"You're my best friend," he says, and even though we aren't usually sweet, I guess today is a day where we are both being sweet with each other.

This time neither of us squirms.

Loving Danny isn't a hypothesis, it is a fact of the universe, and nothing—not even Elsa and Levi—could ever change that.

He looks up to the sky like some snow might start falling down now, just for him.

If I could make that happen for him, I would.

List of Expressions That Danny's Face Makes and What They Mean

- Curved-down lips and sad eyes mean he's worried about something that he doesn't want to talk about.

- Toothy smile and raised eyebrows mean he's excited about a sneaky plan that he hasn't told anyone yet.

- Open lips and wrinkled nose mean he finds something either very gross or totally baffling.

- Closed eyes and pinched mouth mean something hurts and he's trying to wish it away.

- Puffed-out lips and wrinkled forehead mean he's on his way to sadness but could still be stopped.

- Big eyes and closed-mouth smile mean he misses something he used to have and wonders if it will ever come back.

Elsa, Levi, Rachel, and I are looking at clouds on Wednesday afternoon.

Danny is doing another overnight at the hospital because he keeps getting new infections that are building on whatever his main disease is. Mom says that happens with the type of immune problem they're pretty sure Danny has. It doesn't seem fair to me—he already has a really hard sickness, and now because that sickness has made him so weak, he can't fight off any other infections.

I have so many thoughts and questions about how one problem leads to more problems, but I'm trying to forget about questions and infections and even Danny, for a minute or two.

Elsa, Levi, and Rachel are trying to find a relationship between the clouds' shapes and the amount it rains. Elsa has a theory that heart-shaped clouds rain less, and cloud-shaped clouds rain more. Levi has a theory that it is windy for ten minutes before the first raindrop hits.

Rachel has a theory that when she feels weepy, it means it's going to rain.

I'm a scientist, but I like Rachel's theory best of all, so maybe I'm something else besides a scientist, too.

Or maybe I really like Rachel.

"I should do my own project on emotions and weather," Rachel says. "I think my emotions are deeply connected to weather patterns."

"I think you are crazy," Levi mumbles. I can tell that some days he thinks his mom is funny and some days he thinks she's annoying. I wonder if he minds her looking at the clouds with us. For all I know, he minds *me* watching the clouds with him and Elsa. It's hard to say what Levi feels at any one time.

"What do you think, Clover?" Rachel asks, even though it's not my science fair project.

I squint at the clouds and sniff the air. I wiggle my toes and roll my ankles. I look at the sun, at the trees waving in the wind, at the grass's color.

"I don't know," I say. "My ankles don't hurt. I don't think it will rain."

"Maybe we'll never know everything there is to know about the weather," Elsa says. She is furiously taking notes.

"I read that you can make your own psychrometer," I say. "It's a thing that measures humidity in the air." I meant to stay quiet and let Elsa and Levi do their project without me, since I have my own project, and helping them feels like I'm betraying Danny. But I looked up how to forecast the weather, and I found out building a psychrometer is pretty easy. And I guess it sounds cool. It's the kind of thing I'd do if I didn't have my own Very Important Project.

"How will it help our project?" Elsa asks. Rachel turns toward me too. Levi doesn't take his eyes off the sky.

"Humidity can help predict rain." I shrug like it's no big deal, but I love that there's a device you can make in your house that can tell you the future. It makes me feel hopeful about solving all the other mysteries in my life. If we can predict the rain, maybe we can also predict what will happen to Danny. If a couple of kids can make a psychrometer, a bunch of fancy doctors in Vermont can figure out Danny. "I saw it on a website. I'll show you. You just need thermometers and some gauze and a little fan."

"And then you can tell what will happen with the weather?" Elsa asks. "No way."

"Science can solve everything," I say, mostly to myself. Elsa and Levi nod.

"Some things will always remain mysteries!" Rachel says. Levi huffs.

"My mom likes mysteries of the universe," he says. "She says faith comes from mysteries." And I don't see him roll his eyes, but I can hear it. I wish I knew something like that about my mother. I know she likes cooking, like me, and she likes the air conditioner on high. I know she is a really good mom and that when Jake is being hard, she treats herself to a scoop of mint chocolate chip ice cream and an episode of some show about women with big lips and men in suits who kiss too much.

But I don't know what she thinks about the world.

"I thought science had all the answers," I say, turning toward Rachel. "I thought that was the whole point." I make fists with my hands and try not to sound desperate. I don't have time for mysteries. I don't have space for them.

"Sometimes the answer is magic," Rachel says. Her eyebrows are raised and Levi is blushing. "And I don't think it's going to rain today. I don't feel like crying at all."

Magic. I'd written that word down in my book last week, and I keep trying to ignore it, but it keeps popping right back up. I wonder if there's room for science *and* magic. I wonder if both are possible at once.

"Do you really believe in magic?" I ask Rachel. She smiles.

Levi answers for her. "She made it rain once," he says. All this time I thought he didn't believe a word his mom said, but it turns out I don't know Levi very well at all. He looks a little proud now. Sheepish, but proud. Elsa giggles.

"The atmosphere makes it rain!" she says. And I know that, but I want to know more about Rachel's magic.

"You know the clinic I told you about?" Rachel says. "There was science there, and room for faith and religion, too, which are important to me, but I think there was magic too. And art. All things that help us figure out other ways to see the world. I think we need all those things."

I think about Ms. Fitch. When we came back from the aquarium trip, she told us to draw the way the fish looked, but also the way they made us feel.

"So don't draw them the real way?" Brandy asked.

"The way they look and the way they make you feel are both real," Ms. Fitch said. She smiled like she was telling us the world's biggest secret.

"When I was sick—" Rachel starts to speak again, but Levi won't let her finish.

"I don't want to talk about when you were sick anymore," he says. "You already told me all about that." That's when I see the thing Levi and I have in common that's even bigger than the way we like science and logic and Elsa.

He's scared, too. He's scared like me, of the way illness can change everything.

I want Levi to get what he wants, but I'm not ready to let the conversation with Rachel go, so I ask my question quietly. "Isn't magic for little kids? Didn't the doctors make you better?"

Rachel takes a big breath. I can't imagine her being sick. I wonder if she was like Danny—always getting skinnier and paler and shakier and sadder.

"Magic doesn't have to be a big deal," Rachel says at last. "Sometimes it's very, very small. Sometimes it comes and goes. Magic's not like the fairy tales. It's a moment in time. Or a bond between two people. Or a wish that grows into existence. Sometimes it's a thing that's necessary and accessible. Like how we only use a small part of our brains. We don't always access our magic."

"How do you know if something's magic?" I hold my breath, waiting for the answer.

"Magic is love with a twist," Rachel says, seeing my worried face. I hang on to the words and don't let go.

No one says anything for a minute, and I'm worried I ruined the fun of the day with all my questions. But Elsa is always there to fix things.

"That cloud reminds me of you, Clover," she says, pointing at the prettiest cloud. It looks soft enough to sleep on and the sun is shining through it, making it glow all gold and pink and fairylike.

It's the best compliment I've ever gotten.

I think if anyone has magic, it must be Elsa.

And maybe, maybe me.

19

Dad is back from his latest trip for a few days, so on Saturday we have our annual sundae-making competition with Danny's family. Helen was so eager she called every single day this week to confirm, even the days Danny was sickest, which were all the days I didn't have time to visit him.

"Thanks for waiting for me to do the competition," Dad says when we get to their house, loaded down with ice cream flavors and a few of our favorite traditional toppings.

"It's a family thing," I say. "It has to be the whole family." I let Dad hold my hand, even though I usually think it's babyish. Today it's nice.

"Dad is only our family sometimes," Jake says. It's going to be one of those days with Jake. The ones where he says whatever pops into his head, even if it's a little mean or awkward or downright wrong. These aren't the worst days with Jake, but they're hard. He'll comment on the way a stranger looks or tell Mom's friends something rude she said about them behind closed doors.

Dad looks sad at this comment, even though he knows how Jake is.

"That's not how family works!" I say. "Dad's in our family when he's at home *and* when he's on the road."

"I would never want to be a truck driver," Jake says.

"You don't have to be one," I say. I squeeze Dad's hand.

"Well, we're just so pleased you could all make it," Helen says. She looks a little weepy and a little nervous. This is how she looks all the time now.

Danny promised he wouldn't tell anyone about our new hypothesis, but I'm suspicious he let something slip to his mother. She's looking at me in a brand-new way, and it's making me itchy. She hugs me three times in three minutes, and that is too many hugs.

The second we're inside, she starts snapping pictures of me and Danny, and no matter how many times he tells her to stop, she won't.

"You can see me anytime," he says with his arms crossed over his chest. "You don't need a million photos of me." I wonder what Ms. Fitch would say about the photos. I think Helen is taking pictures of the way she wants things to be, more than the way they are. Ms. Fitch would approve, I think. "Art isn't a research paper," she said last week. "There's no right or wrong. It's about the things you want and miss and love and wish you knew."

I hope Helen's photos show her what she wants to see.

Last night Danny called me, but I could barely hear him. His voice was hoarse and small. He didn't sound any-thing like regular Danny. He said something was wrong with his throat and that he had a brand-new infection in his ears.

He begged me to come over. I did. He felt better after about half an hour.

"See, you're fixing me," he said, but I disagreed.

"I'm like cold medicine," I said, pulling out my note-book to show him the patterns. "You feel better for a little, but then you feel worse. I don't make you not sick, I just fix your symptoms."

But Danny didn't want to hear it. "We don't know how it works," he said. "That's why we have to go to Vermont. To find out."

He's right. We don't know if I'm like cold medicine or if I have to be within five feet of him for the rest of our lives to keep him well.

We need more answers. And we aren't getting them

from any of the doctors on Danny's "team."

"I want to remember every wonderful day," Helen says, snapping another photo and saying the word *wonderful* like it's a dessert she's licking up. "Stand closer to Danny, Clover."

I give Danny a look. "Did you tell her?" I whisper.

Danny shrugs.

"You promised!"

"I didn't tell her, but she kind of guessed on her own. You're not the only scientist. Mom knows stuff too."

"Did you ask her about Vermont again?" I ask. "Vermont is more important than me anyway."

"You know she won't let me travel. She says I'll get even more infections if I'm in new environments."

We should be whispering more quietly, but everyone's talking over everyone else, so we're pretty sure no one's listening to us. Jake is being very loud; he's a great distraction sometimes.

"We have to get there on our own," Danny says.

I'd do absolutely anything to find out what's wrong, and I'm pretty sure the clinic is the only hope we have. We will figure out a way.

"You two stop whispering and come get your ice cream!" Helen says. She's stopped taking pictures for long enough to fill everyone's bowls with three scoops each of different flavors.

We've been having a sundae-making competition every year for my whole life. It started when Mom was pregnant with me and Helen was pregnant with Danny and they both were craving ice cream, but wildly different kinds. Mom wanted mint chocolate chip with pretzels and whipped cream on top. Helen wanted vanilla and every kind of sauce—chocolate, caramel, strawberry. She wanted nuts and cherries and a banana underneath it all, like a boat carrying a very sweet load of cargo.

The sundae-making competition is the best day of the year.

But this year Jake is on his rampage and Helen has nervous bird-energy and Danny's illness is so large it feels tight in the kitchen.

Every year Helen gives everyone three scoops and we have full use of the kitchen to put any topping we want onto the sundae. I won last year with a peanut-butter-and-every-kind-of-jelly-ever concoction. Mom won the year before with bacon bits and maple syrup.

We grab our bowls and Helen wipes her brow like she's all worn out from the effort of scooping. For a moment, the day feels very nearly good and normal.

Danny leans against the fridge, surveying the toppings on the counter.

"If you need to lie down—" Helen whispers into Danny's ear. We all hear her, and Danny waves her off. His eyes are bright and he doesn't look tired at all. He barely looks sick except for how skinny he is. "Was this too much for you after your hard night last night?" Danny wants to be mad, I think, but he stays cheery.

"Don't try to trick me into forfeiting!" he says, and Helen laughs and takes a picture of Danny and me feeding each other a scoop of pre-sundae-ed ice cream.

Mom looks through their refrigerator and pulls out fruits and vegetables, and I decide to make my sundae a soup, so I start mashing up the ice cream.

"How is ice cream when it's microwaved?" I ask. "Like, warm ice cream? Could that be good?"

"No assists!" Ross says. He's always in charge of the rules. The room's full of people but also full of warmth. There's the sun, of course. There's always the sun. But there's also the way we all know each other and the smell of hot fudge on the stove and the oldies station that Helen's singing along to and Danny buzzing around without even a sniffle or a limp.

There's enough good stuff in the room that I feel like I can relax for a minute. It's almost like last year, which was perfect.

"Danny, if you die by next year, can I make your sundae, too?" Jake says. "If you die, can I make two sundaes?" His hands are covered in ice cream and sprinkles and a sheen of butter. There are sprinkles in his hair. He's a Jake-sundae, and it was so cute a minute ago but now it's all wrong.

The day turns so fast I lose my breath.

Helen drops her bowl of ice cream.

Mom rushes to Jake's side like she might be able to shove the words back in his mouth.

I look at the floor and wish myself into the moment before.

Danny sputters a laugh, but it's the ugly kind. A cackle, really. Ross shushes him and I know the competition is pretty much over before it began.

No one's said anything about Danny dying.

"Jake, that's rude," I say, but my mind is rushing with a thousand other scary thoughts.

Usually when Jake says something, it's because he's over-heard someone else saying something and he's repeating it.

I wonder if Jake heard Mom or Dad say something about Danny and . . . dying.

That's not possible, though. My throat's dry and my head hurts, but there's no way anyone could think Danny's going to die.

Dying is something old people and bald kids in bad movies do. Dying is something in books.

I put my hand over my heart to calm it down. *No one's dying,* I tell my heart. *I'm here, fixing him,* I tell my heart.

We're going to get to Vermont. We're going to find out what's wrong. We're going to see snow, I tell my sad, aching, beat-up heart.

"What are you telling your children about my son?" Helen says. Mom steps back. That's not what she was expecting. She's ready to give Jake yet another speech on what is and is not okay to say about other people. But Helen's not mad at Jake. She's mad at Mom.

"You know Jake," Mom says. "He doesn't think about things the same way the other kids do. He has his own ways of processing—"

"But what are you saying that's making him think Danny might die?" Helen says. She says the word *die* like she's been practicing saying it out loud for weeks in her mirror. It's a little too forceful.

"Stop saying *die*!" I say. I'm even louder than Helen, and Danny gives me a look.

"It's fine, everyone," he says. "Jake didn't mean it."

"Stop talking about me," Jake says. He doesn't like when he hears his name being thrown around but can't quite understand why. It happens a lot, and it always means the start of a tantrum. Now would be a terrible time for a tantrum.

"Danny's getting better," Helen says. "Look at him. He looks wonderful. Like our little boy."

"You look really good, Danny," Mom says.

"Danny's fine!" I say. "We're figuring it out!" I stop myself before I say anything else.

"I'm sure the doctors are figuring everything out," Dad says in his calm voice. I'm glad he's here; he's good at sounding relaxed when things are stressful.

"I feel great right now," Danny says. "I know Jake didn't mean it." His voice shakes, though, and I wonder if Jake's words scared Danny a little too.

I take another bite of my soupy ice cream and Danny does the same. We want the day back, but I don't think it's coming back, so we might as well eat as much ice cream as we can.

"Jake, you want some M&Ms?" Danny asks. "You want to try putting gum on the ice cream? I've always wanted to try that."

Jake starts to wail.

Jake cries like a baby when he's upset, and it brings me back to when I was four and he was brand-new and I'd be up all night listening to him screech in his crib. It was a terrible sound then and it's terrible now, too. Danny covers his ears.

"It's okay, Jakey," I say. "We're having fun!" I do a little jig in front of him. I stick out my tongue and try to feed him ice cream from my own spoon.

"It's not fun! I'm not having fun!" Jake screams. His arms start helicoptering and his legs are stomping on the floor. The kitchen shakes a little, even though Jake's tiny. He's powerful. He's an earthquake, destroying us all.

Helen hides her face in her hands.

"I think you need to go," Ross says. He says so little most of the time that it's extra awful when he says something pointed and painful.

"Don't make them leave," Danny says. He puts a hand on the top of Jake's head, like that might help the situation, but it only makes Jake worse. He pushes Danny. It's not powerful or on purpose. It doesn't do much but make Danny trip a little. But it's enough to make Helen leave the room and enough to make Mom and Dad gather us up and pull us right out of there.

I don't have time to say good-bye to Danny, and I know he's worried that he's going to start feeling sick again the minute I'm out the door.

It was supposed to be a wonderful day, the best kind of day, but instead it is a terrible day.

⌒⌒

When we get home, Mom gives Jake a Popsicle.

"I wanted ice cream," he says.

"Well," Mom says. We don't have anything else to say.

But I wonder about what Helen asked. I've never heard

anyone talk about Danny and dying. Not even Danny, who will say anything about everything. Dying and Danny aren't words that go together. Not ever. I can't even think the two words in my brain at the same time. One comes in and I have to get it all the way out before the other word can arrive, on its own. They're like trains, timed one after the other, minutes apart. And my brain is a crowded station.

I ask for a Popsicle of my own, but we're all out.

"Jake needed it," Mom says. "You understand, right, Clover?"

And I do understand, but I am missing the sweetness I was supposed to have today. I'm missing the fun and the taste of sugar and the things I thought I knew for sure.

The next morning, Mom tells me I've been quiet since
yesterday.

"I know," I say. "You don't have to tell me when I'm
being quiet."

"Attitude, Clover," she says, and I want to say something
mean about Jake and his attitude yesterday, but I keep my
mouth shut. It's Dad's last morning before he goes on the
road again tonight, and I like those mornings to be perfect.
Or close to perfect.

My secret, secret thought is that if the mornings before
Dad leaves aren't pretty close to perfect, he might not come
back.

It's a thought I know isn't true, but when I'm alone at night in my bed, I think it somehow might be a little true. Sometimes something that isn't true can *feel* true.

"How long are you gone this time?" I ask Dad.

"Short trip, only three days. Then I'll have a big trip up north. All the way through New England. That one will be a little longer."

"Like, um, Vermont?" I ask. My mind is spinning. I should have thought of it before. My dad goes up north all the time. He probably passes through Vermont multiple times a year.

"Massachusetts, New Hampshire, Vermont, Maine," he says. "Lots of beautiful places. I'll pick you up a snow globe from each one, how's that?"

"And you'll get me a T-shirt from each one," Jake says. He doesn't ever say it as a question. It's a rule—if Dad gets me something, he has to get Jake something too.

"Of course," Dad says.

I try to keep my voice from shaking. I try to keep my hands and knees from shaking too. "How big is Vermont?"

"One of the smaller states," Dad says.

"When do you leave for that trip?" I'm probably asking a few too many questions, so this will be my last one. They'll start getting suspicious otherwise.

"Right after your birthday!" Dad says. "Don't you worry.

I'll be here for the big day. Eleven is an important year."

"You said seven was an important year," Jake says. He will always remember every single thing anyone says, so we all have to be careful to say only things we mean. Dad's always forgetting that, and Jake's always calling him out on it.

Today it makes us all laugh. That's how I know my family's going to be okay. Even after a terrible day like yesterday, we still smile at each other.

I wonder if Danny's family is okay today, or if the upset from yesterday hung around them, haunting them.

My question is answered in the afternoon. Danny is in his front yard. He has set up a lawn chair, and he has a big ugly sunhat on too. I know for a fact Helen has slathered him in sunblock.

I make a note in my notebook. Temperature. Direction of the sun. Chemicals on his body. Hour of the day. Humidity percentages.

I know we have a sturdy hypothesis, but it's not one I like, and it's not one that tells me what's wrong with him, so my work isn't done. I want to find anything else that might have to do with Danny's illness. We have to go to Vermont so I can show them all my research and have them shake my hand and tell me I'm really quite a scientist. Those fancy doctors will see how I didn't give up and I didn't stop at one question and I didn't get lazy after finding a few answers.

And then they'll tell me, "Clover, we've got this now. We can fix Danny."

I walk over to Danny's lawn chair and try to startle him. It is probably a bad, dangerous thing, but I want us to be able to have fun still, in some of the ways we used to.

"Boo!" I say, right into his ear. He jumps in his seat and smiles and there it is, there we are, Danny and Clover.

"Practicing for Halloween tomorrow?" Danny asks. I'd forgotten about Halloween. We don't usually go trick-or-treating—it freaks Jake out, and I like to stay home and watch scary movies with Danny. I guess we won't be doing that tomorrow. I'll hand out candy with Jake and that will be good, too.

"Your parents aren't coming outside, right?" Danny says.

The smile is gone. There's nervousness instead.

"Not right now."

"And no Jake?" He looks around me, peering over my right hip, which is eye level with him.

"I think he's playing video games," I say.

"I'm allowed to see you," he says. "Because they know what you do for me. How you help me. But I can't see the rest of your family."

A single cough comes out of his mouth. We pause,

waiting to see if there's more coughing to come, but there's not.

"Jake didn't mean it," I say.

"He sort of did," Danny says. "I don't mind. But my parents . . . they want me to think positively. We went to this workshop last night at the community center. 'The Power of Thought.' I don't know. They think it will help."

"Jake didn't know what he was saying." I want to know more about the workshop and why they're willing to take Danny to the community center but not up to Vermont. I can't understand why they think a workshop could help but they won't try Rachel's clinic.

"I'm really sick," Danny says. "That much is true. And it's not impossible that I'll—"

"I'm fixing you!" I say. I don't believe in the power of positive thought, but I do believe in stopping him before he finishes a sentence that I can't stand to hear.

"You have school and stuff." Danny shrugs. He looks sad. Maybe Jake really did upset him. Maybe it's not only his parents that don't want him to see my family. Maybe he doesn't want to see them either.

"My parents know you're going to be okay," I say.

"No one knows that, Clover," he says. He is getting sadder and sadder, drooping in the sun.

"My parents want me to see you less and your parents

don't want you to see my family and I don't get any of it," I say. "We have to do something."

Danny looks over at my house and I wonder if he can see my parents moving inside of it—Mom helping Dad pack, Jake glued to the couch, everything the same as it's always been but so, so different too. "All that matters is that we can see each other," he says.

I try to agree with him.

"Hey, is the sun okay for you?" I step closer to him. Soon, my powers should be kicking in and he should be feeling better.

"Vitamin D," Danny says. "Doctor said it was worth a try."

"What hurts today?" I ask, knowing the answer just by looking at him.

"Stomach again. Cough seems okay. I'm tired."

"Here." I put a hand on his knee. I let it rest there, and there's a heat between my palm and his skin. Maybe it's Florida heat or maybe it's something scientific or maybe, maybe it's magic. "Helping?"

"Helping," he says. Soon his body relaxes and I try his other knee, his elbows, his shoulder.

I can feel Helen and Ross watching us from inside. The lawn chair fits both of us pretty well, and the sun feels delicious, for once.

"Did I tell you that Levi, Elsa, and I made you a blizzard?" I ask. I keep meaning to bring over the snowflakes, to hang them around Danny's house, but every day Danny has some new bit of sickness, and I forget all about the snow.

"I don't know what that means," Danny says.

"Rachel, Levi's mom, says snow is healing. That's part of what's so great about the clinic in Vermont."

"My grandfather never saw snow either," Danny says. I want him to snap out of his bad mood, but it is simply not happening.

I've never seen Elsa in a bad mood. She doesn't seem to get in them, and I love that. I want to be around her sunniness. But as soon as I realize that's what I want, I'm embarrassed.

I try to shut my brain up about Elsa.

"I thought you didn't know much about your grandfather."

"I didn't. I asked a lot of questions, though. I think he had what I have. I'm pretty positive. Mom says they couldn't figure out what was wrong and the symptoms kept changing. Then she started crying and said Grandpa didn't have someone like you to save him."

"Oh." I don't know what to say. I take out my notebook. It's safer there.

"Write down that he never saw snow and he mystified

doctors and that sometimes your body attacks itself and they don't know exactly why. Write down all the ways we're the same." Danny is getting worked up. His voice is cracking and he's rubbing his eyes like maybe they're about to release a flash flood of tears.

"You know what the difference between you and your grandfather really is?" I say. Danny doesn't respond. He doesn't think there is a difference, but he doesn't see what I see. "I think the thing between us is more than science. I think it's magic."

"You don't believe in magic," Danny mumbles, but I swear I see a light in his eyes and a lift of his lips.

"Magic's just love with a twist," I say, and I wonder if I sound like Rachel.

Danny nods. It's a small nod, but it's better than nothing. I can see him thinking about the word *magic*. Maybe that is the only word for what we have between us.

"Clover?" His voice is quiet. Maybe his parents are listening in, or maybe his throat hurts, or maybe this is how Danny is now.

"Yep?"

"I'm really scared."

I think my heart must stop beating, because everything pauses for a moment.

I can't tell him not to be scared, because I am too.

"I have a plan," I say. I'm excited to say the words out loud for the first time, and I try to see that same happiness in his face, but the fear is hiding it. "I know how to get to Vermont."

"My parents said no. I told you that."

"We're not going to get permission," I say. "We're just going to go."

My notebook has a calendar on the back page, and I use my pen to circle the day after my birthday—November 6. It is only a week away. "This is the day," I say.

"Your birthday's the fifth," Danny says. "Just have a party on the fifth." A few months ago, I think Danny would know exactly what I was trying to tell him already, but his sickness has made him a little unfocused and distracted. I have to get him to listen.

"November sixth is the day we're going to Vermont," I say. I tell him about my dad's trip up north and the space on his truck where I know we can hole up for the ride. "I've done some math." I put my shoulders back, proud of the way I use math and science and hope and love all at once. "According to my math, a drive straight from here to the Somerset Clinic would be about twenty hours. But Dad makes a bunch of stops for deliveries and also has to take breaks to sleep and rest and have coffee. So I've calculated that we will be at the Somerset Clinic on November eighth, by dinnertime."

I write down numbers as I talk to Danny—how many

hours Dad sleeps, how long it takes to unload and reload the truck, how many times Dad says he stops for coffee, and I add them all up in front of him.

"Won't he find us eventually? Won't our parents be worried?" Danny asks. It is the hardest part about our plan. I know our parents will freak out when they find we are missing.

"Dad will probably find us before we get all the way there," I say. "And if he does, we have to hope it will be too late for him to turn around and bring us home. He'll have to finish his job, and we can't exactly walk home, so we'll get to go with him."

Danny nods. I think he's starting to understand how great my science brain is for planning and scheming and calculating. I'm starting to see how great my science brain is too.

"And our parents worrying?"

"I can tell my parents I'm meeting Elsa early, to help her test some morning weather."

"And me?" Danny asks. But his solution is even easier.

"All you have to do is tell your parents you're with me," I say, "and they won't worry at all."

Danny smiles. "That's true."

It's all coming together—maps and numbers and the Someday Suitcase and the Somerset Clinic and my epic plan and my science brain.

"Wait," Danny says. "We get to Vermont November eighth?"

"Yeah."

November 8 is the day of the science fair. Danny knows because it's important to me and he was going to try to feel well enough to come.

"It's perfect," I say, wanting Danny's worried, guilty face to go away. "It's the conclusion of my science fair project on the day of the science fair!"

"But you're missing the fair."

"Ms. Mendez says the fair isn't the point of the experiments. She says some people won't have conclusions at the fair, even, because science is our effort to control the unpredictable. She says scientists sit back and let the world happen in its own time; they don't try to force something."

There's a long pause before Danny's face changes, but when it finally does, it turns into my very favorite Danny look. Eyes crinkly, mouth wide and pushing his cheeks up, chin jutted up at the sky. Pure happiness.

"The end of the experiment," Danny says with a big nod.

"Vermont," I say, nodding back.

"We have a plan," Danny says, and as much as I liked saying the words, they sound even better coming from him.

21

"I hear you're all very focused on your science fair projects," Ms. Fitch says when we're in class on Monday one week and one day before the big fair.

The whole class nods. Elsa and Levi keep looking out the window to see if it's raining. They have predicted a rainfall at noon today, and if it doesn't happen, they have to reassess their data. Brandy and Marco have cat scratches all up and down their arms because Brandy insisted on doing a project about her cat. José smells like glue and keeps doodling pictures of cars on every piece of scrap paper around. Paloma can't stop yawning because she's staying up late every night for her astronomy project.

"Remember how after the aquarium we drew pictures of fish and how they made us feel?" Ms. Fitch asks. Brandy presses on one of her scratches. Paloma yawns again. I wonder what Danny would have drawn if he'd been in class that day. "Well, I'm going to give you free rein of the classroom. All the craft supplies. All the clay and paints and glitter and scraps of paper and yarn you could ever need. I want you to make something that tells us about your project. Or maybe you can even make something that might help you with your project. Sometimes art is about beauty and sometimes it's about necessity. Did you know art has a little bit of everything in it? Science and math and literature are all a part of art."

Elsa and Levi crane their necks. It's 11:50 and there's no rain in sight.

"Can't we just go work on our projects?" Marco asks. He is very serious about winning the science fair. His brother won it last year, and his sister two years before that.

"Sometimes you need to turn something over and upside down to really see it," Ms. Fitch says. "I think if you take a break from looking at your project through the science lens, you might be surprised at all the new things you see."

Marco sighs. Paloma yawns. Brandy asks if maybe she should go to the nurse about one particularly nasty scratch on her elbow.

I go through the plan for November 6 again in my head. Get out of bed super early in the morning, before the sun comes up, right before Dad gets on the road. I know where the extra keys are, so we can sneak into the truck with no problem at all. Stay very quiet. Make sure Danny doesn't snore. Sneak out for bathroom breaks when Dad stops for bathroom breaks. Hope our parents don't worry too much.

"Don't get so stuck on finding solutions that you lose sight of everything else," Ms. Fitch says. "That's what art's for. So that you don't lose sight of everything else."

Elsa gives me a look, a serious one. She thinks Ms. Fitch is talking about me and the way I can sometimes see only Danny and nothing else.

I wander the art room, looking for something that will make me see my experiment in a whole new way.

"I think you're going to win," Levi says. I hadn't noticed him behind me, so I jump a little at the sound of his voice.

"You do?" I ask. And for a second I forget that I won't be at the fair, that I can't win. I picture myself with the trophy—it's a shiny goblet that they engrave the winner's name into. I think I'd put it in our living room so that no one would ever forget I'm a scientist, including myself.

"Obviously," Levi says, like it's so obvious it doesn't require any explanation at all.

"I want to win," I say. I'm surprised by the words. I

didn't think I cared about anything but curing Danny. It feels a little bit good, to care about something that's mine.

My heart sinks a little. Because I can't win if I'm not here.

I almost tell Levi my whole plan, but I'm too scared of getting caught, of something going wrong. So instead I smile really big. "Thanks for saying that," I say, looking him right in the eye so he knows how much I mean it.

Levi grabs behind me to get some string.

"I want to make a kite," he says. "Elsa wants to make a rain bucket. Do you know where the clay is?"

I laugh because Levi and Elsa already see the world in beautiful, strange, upside-down ways. I point to the clay and tell Levi I think a kite and a rain bucket will make their project complete. He hands me a hunk of clay too.

"You'll figure out something good to do with this," he says.

❧

I sit with Elsa and Levi, but I tune them out, which they don't seem to mind. They're both hard at work—Levi drawing alien shapes on the paper for his kite and Elsa trying to find the perfect curve for a rain bucket. The rain they predicted doesn't come, but neither of them notice. That's what art does; it lets your mind focus on something else.

I roll the clay around in my hands for a while. I

contemplate all the watercolors in the middle of the table and try to pick my favorite shade. I'm tempted to take out my Danny notebook, but I don't. I close my eyes. I turn everything upside down and inside out. I forget Vermont and immune disorders and sick grandfathers and trucks.

I let my hands do the thinking.

It feels good, to let go of numbers and charts and theories.

My hands take over.

"Pretty," Elsa says when the bell rings and art class is over. I look down at what I've done. I half expect to see a sculpture of Danny's head or a big heart for how much I love him.

Instead, I have made a trophy. It looks just like the one they give to the science fair winner, only smaller and with a little snowflake carved on one side, and my name on the other.

It's only my name, not Danny's, and even though I sculpted it and I engraved it, I'm surprised.

Ms. Fitch comes by to pick up anything any of us made from clay so she can put it in the kiln.

She lifts my trophy up and looks at the way it swoops at the top and balloons at the bottom.

"You decide whether or not you win," she says, in her singsongy, supersmart voice. "You know whether or not you did your very best on your project. I love this, Clover."

I've never been much of an artist, but when Ms. Fitch says those words, I feel like one, for a moment.

I add the trophy to the list of what to pack for our trip. It will be out of the kiln in a few days, and I won't have time to paint it, but I'll ask Ms. Fitch if I can take it to show Danny. Really, though, it's me who needs it. It's silly, and it's selfish, but on November 8 I'll know I did everything I possibly could to be the scientist that Danny deserves.

List of Things to Bring to Vermont

- Sweaters
- Bananas
- Water bottles
- Goldfish
- Cough syrup
- Advil
- A thermos of Helen's special tea
- Books
- Camera
- Sandwiches
- A map of where the Somerset Clinic is
- Thermometer
- Cookies
- Trail mix
- A blanket
- My research notebook
- Danny's doctor's phone number, just in case
- My trophy

22

The next day, Ms. Mendez wants to know how our science fair projects are going, and I don't know how to answer.

"I figured out a lot," I say, and maybe it's my imagination, but I think everyone in class starts doodling in their notebooks or finding other places to look. It turns out no one at all wants to hear me talk about Danny. But it's hard not to talk about him all the time. "It's really coming together."

"Wow, Clover. That's great news. Want to tell us a little more?"

I have about a million things I could tell her about Danny and maybe magic and the Somerset Clinic and my notebook filled with facts and theories and the big circle around November 6, which is less than one week away.

But I know to be careful. I think before I answer.

"I think I've found that once you answer one question, about a hundred more questions pop up," I say. "So an experiment never really ends. It just . . . shifts."

"Evolves," Ms. Mendez says, nodding and smiling and making me feel extra smart.

"Yeah. My experiment has evolved," I say.

"That's a great lesson to have learned, Clover," Ms. Mendez says. "Sometimes you answer questions you didn't even know you were asking."

I love how Ms. Mendez understands everything. I could hug her. "Exactly!" I say. I grin and wonder if there's any way to ask if magic and science have ever collided before, but I decide to be safe; I'll wait and ask that question at the clinic. In Vermont, Danny and I can finally be totally honest about everything.

I wish we could leave right now, but I'd hate to miss science class.

We're going to talk more about pollination and how it relates to symbiosis. I can't miss that.

"I've learned that we can predict some things, sometimes, but not all the things all the time," Elsa says. "I guess I thought I'd be sure of everything when we were done. But

I'm not more sure. I'm just more . . . um . . ." Elsa trails off, trying to find the right word.

"Informed," Levi finishes for her, and I feel a deep ache for Danny finishing my sentences.

"That's a life lesson, too, isn't it?" Ms. Mendez says. She sounds a little dreamy. "Science teaches us about the world and also ourselves. It shows us certainties and limitations to certainties." I think she looks at me for an extra pause, like there's a lesson I'm supposed to learn, more than everyone else.

"And it was fun!" Elsa says.

"Fun is great, too," Ms. Mendez says. I think I love Ms. Mendez, and I definitely love science. I love it more than math or baking, which I also love. In math and baking things turn out the way you want them to, or else you've failed. Either the bread rises or it doesn't. Either the numbers even out, or they don't. But in science, like with art, even when you're wrong, you're right. As long as you're trying, you're doing your job.

Magic's that way too, I think. I hide a secret smile.

Brandy says she learned even more about cats than she already knew, which was a lot, and that she learned she wants to learn more about cats. Other kids talk about how hard it was to remember to have control factors and to do the experiments the same way every time. I think the kids who made the solar panel car will probably win the science fair, even though solar panel cars are boring and everyone knows their parents helped. But that doesn't matter.

I know I can't win. I know I can't be there. And it hurts, but I also know I learned the most important thing of all:

Until it's proven false, anything is possible.

Even magic.

~⁓

"You coming over?" Elsa says when we get out of school that afternoon. Levi is deep in a comic book, walking and reading at the same time. Elsa has to keep steering him in the right direction and yelling at him not to cross the street without looking.

It's nice, to see the way everyone takes care of each other.

"I think I'm going to head to Danny's," I say, even though I'd like to go with Elsa and Levi. Elsa grabs Levi's shoulder and makes him turn right, out of the path of a bunch of second graders walking in the opposite direction.

It's such a nice gesture, and Levi doesn't even really know she's doing it.

"Hey, Levi?" I say. "Elsa's saving you. I hope you realize that." He looks up from his comic book and finally sees the world around him zooming by. He startles.

"Oh," he says, but there's so much more to the *oh* than just that sound. "Thanks."

And I know it doesn't sound like much, but he sounds like he really means it.

"That's what friends are for," Elsa says in this singsong voice, and she says it with a sort of smirk and a nudge, but it hits me right in the heart.

And like that, I know I have to tell them.

Not everything. But the plan.

It feels good to tell them, because it's all I can think about, and it feels like I'm finally being honest, to say it out loud.

"We're going to the Somerset Clinic," I say. I tell them about the truck and show them my list of things to pack, and when I'm done talking, I feel like I can finally breathe again.

"That sounds scary," Levi says.

"That sounds amazing," Elsa says.

"It's going to work," I say, as loudly and as certainly as I can. "Plus, I bet we'll see snow!"

"You can add our psychrometer to your list," Levi says. "So that you can make sure the snow is coming. We'll give you all our snow-related research."

"But you need it for the fair!" I say.

Elsa and Levi exchange a look. My heart expands.

"This is more important," Levi says. Elsa nods. They are serious and sure. They are amazing friends. I'm too surprised to even say thank you, so I just nod too.

I take out my notebook and add the psychrometer to the list.

Just like Ms. Mendez said, sometimes scientists stumble upon reasons for their experiments way after the experiments have started.

Ms. Mendez says science is what connects us all, and I guess this means she's right.

23

There is a star piñata. It's pink and red and yellow and swinging like a big clock. There are cookies too, and cake, and a mess of chips and pretzels and oniony dips that are already dripping onto the crinkly paper tablecloths Mom always gets for birthdays.

I thought I didn't really want a party. I'm too focused on what happens after the party, when we sneak into Dad's truck and steal away with him. But Mom and Dad insisted, so here we are, me and Danny, waiting for my birthday to begin so that it can end.

He hasn't said happy birthday yet, and I'm trying not to be mad about it. I think he's forgotten—not that it's my birthday, of course, the purple streamers make that obvious—but that my birthday matters at all.

"Maybe we can sneak out in the middle," he says, like that's a thing I would definitely want.

I haven't told him about the flutter of happiness in my stomach and how much I like the purple streamers and that I'm looking forward to seeing Elsa and Levi and cracking open my piñata. I can't wait for Dad to finish up his errands and come home with a special cake with my name on it. I didn't want a party, but now that it's here, new feelings are popping up without my permission. He doesn't know that I'm hoping my parents got me a unicycle and an ice-cream cake. Lately, Danny doesn't know much about my life outside of him, but that will change, after the Somerset Clinic. I'll make a list of things that I didn't get to talk to him about because it would have seemed too selfish when he was sick.

"I can't sneak out of my own party," I say with a smile, even though underneath I'm sad at how little Danny is thinking about me on my birthday.

It feels like everyone from Mr. Yetur's class arrives all at once.

Elsa hugs me around my middle and squeals into my ear. Danny steps back but not too much. He's close. I can feel his closeness the same way I feel my own feelings.

"BIRTHDAY GIRL!" Elsa says, pulling back and

examining me, like I might have changed in between yesterday and today, ten and eleven. Maybe I have. I feel different, at least.

"It's not a big deal," I say, but it's starting to feel like one.

"And Danny's here!" Elsa says. Danny does a funny wave and Elsa mirrors it with too hard a laugh. Danny shrugs, and I wonder if he's here because it's my birthday or because he's afraid of what symptom would hit if he were home.

I shouldn't think that about my best friend.

"Hey, aren't you sick?" Brandy asks. Her nose wrinkles and she puts her hands over her mouth like she's nervous about catching what he has.

"Not today," Danny says.

"So you can come to parties but not to school?" Brandy says. Elsa is trying to secure a tiara to my head and Mom's bringing me a slice of pizza, but all I can think of is how to get Danny out of this conversation, because I know he's hating it.

"Maybe I'll come back to school soon," Danny says. But if this party is any indication, it's the last thing he'd want to do.

"You're probably too behind," Brandy says. She has a reputation for saying rude things that she doesn't realize are rude. Maybe it would have been funny a year ago, but

Danny's not finding it funny today. His face is turning red and he's staring at me like I have some birthday-girl power to make it stop.

"I'm staying caught up," Danny says, but it's not really true. Helen and Ross aren't making him do homework, and he's usually too tired to do work. He probably is behind.

"It would be weird for you to come back now, though," Brandy says.

"New subject!" Elsa says, but she doesn't have a new subject, so then we're all quiet and uncomfortable. My body is swaying between the two groups of people, my two lives. I feel a little like I'm one of the girls, as if I belong with Elsa and Brandy and the rest of my class. And I've never felt that I don't one hundred percent belong with Danny before, so it feels itchy and strange.

But also a little nice.

I don't want to have to choose. I want to be both. I want to be Elsa's friend and Danny's. I want to be a fifth-grade girl and a magical symbiotic creature.

"Clover! Play Taboo with us!" Paloma says. She's never asked me to do anything with her ever. I look at Danny. He's a little dazed and a little overwhelmed, but he waves me off.

"Go," he says. "I'll hang in the living room. I'm good." He puts on a smile that I know is taking him some effort.

"I want to play too!" Elsa calls, and she drags me to the kitchen table, where Mom's set up a few board games and even more desserts. Jake's on the floor being good with a brownie in one hand and a gaming device in the other. He almost blends into our beige tiles.

"Can I be on your team?" Paloma asks. I look around to see who she's talking to, but she's talking to me.

"Me too, me too!" Brandy says.

"Clover and I are best friends, so we have to be on the same team," Elsa says. Brandy and Paloma and the other kids nod like they already knew that, and I guess it's official.

My heart pounds and I look to see if Danny heard. He didn't. He's headed toward a big bowl of chips.

"What about Levi?" I say, even though I should be telling her I already have a best friend. Levi's taken up a patch of floor next to Jake, and they actually look happy there together, on the floor, out of the way.

"Levi's great, but he's not my best-best friend," Elsa says. "Not in the same way. I mean, look at him. He doesn't really want a best friend the same way I do."

Levi's frowning at Jake's video game, and he's got brownie all around his mouth. He's not interested in joining the rest of the party.

I look for Danny again and can see him in the next room. He's busy dipping and chomping. I still don't say what I should say.

Maybe there are different kinds of best friends, I think for one second before I feel too guilty to keep thinking it.

"Levi's best friend is his video games," Elsa says.

"Right," I say, and we crack up, me and Elsa. Her laugh sounds like piano trills, and it hangs on hard and fast. The more she laughs, the more I laugh, and it gets out of control quickly. Out-of-control laughing feels excellent.

Plus, it turns out we're amazing at Taboo.

An hour later Dad shows up with a cake with three layers. It's covered in sugar roses and he puts his hands on his waist after uncovering it, like it's a tree he cut down or a huge fish he caught.

I'm mostly just happy to see Dad, but the cake looks pretty wonderful too.

"Wow," I say.

"I thought you deserved something extra special," he says, and I think my birthday wish will be that we get more days where Dad is home.

But then I remember I have to reserve my birthday wish for Danny and making him better. For an instant I wonder if Danny's still okay in the other room, but Paloma is hanging on to my elbow and bouncing up and down, telling me how pretty the cake is, and I'm still feeling sparkly and special from Elsa calling me her best friend. So I don't check on Danny. I stay right here.

"You're a great kid," Dad says in his crunchy, crackly,

about-to-cry voice. "You've been through a lot, and you've grown up a lot and we wanted your birthday to be special. And fun." He pats my head, and it's embarrassing but nice too. Everyone's clamoring for a piece of cake, and Dad leans down, close to my ear. He knows I won't want everyone to hear everything he has to say. "You're not having enough fun lately, Clover," he says.

True things go right from my ears to my heart and dig little holes there. Truth holes.

This sentence makes a whole bunch of truth holes all at once. He's right. It's not fun, taking care of Danny. It turns out magic isn't very fun at all, actually.

I hate that Danny's not the fun part of my life right now. He has always been the funnest part.

On my ninth birthday he dressed up like a clown and performed a circus for me with a neighborhood dog. Last year he made the whole cafeteria sing "Happy Birthday." I blushed so hard I thought I'd never go back to my regular color.

I finally look for him. The memory of my ninth birthday makes me miss him, makes me want him near.

"Danny?" I say.

"That cake is amazing!" Elsa says. "Your dad is so cool! Can I have a rose? Best friends get roses, right?"

"Right, right," I say, too scared to tell her she can't be my best friend because I have Danny, and he has to be my best friend, always. Even if it's not fun sometimes.

"Danny?" I call again.

"It's your turn at Taboo!" Paloma says. Elsa and I have been winning, and when we do she gives me this special smile, like every win means something about us and our friendship. I let it feel good. I let it feel so good I forgot to make sure Danny was close by.

"Where's Danny?" I ask Dad, but he gives me a serious look like I didn't listen to his Very Important Comment about how I'm not having enough fun.

"I'm sure he's catching up with friends," Dad says. "He must miss everyone. Enjoy your cake, Clo."

I walk into the living room and down to the basement. There are other kids everywhere, but no Danny.

I keep calling out his name, but it doesn't matter because he can't hear it. I know he's back home, watching the shadows of the party through his window and wishing it would end, at the same exact moment I'm wishing it could go on all night.

I leave my own party.

I don't want to, but I have to.

Rachel forgot to tell me that magic is a responsibility. That magic is a thing you have to live up to. A thing you have to prove you're worthy of.

No one blocks the door. No one even sees me go.

Danny's on his couch, where Danny always is. I think the couch would look strange without him on it now. He's part of the pattern.

"You left," I say.

"You didn't even know I was there." The difference between me and Danny—there are many, but the one I'm thinking of now—is that Danny expects to be seen and I don't.

"No one knows that I'm not there right now," I say. "And it's my actual birthday."

"So that makes it okay for you to forget about me?"

"I can't forget about you!" I say. I boom. I've never boomed before. "I can't care about anything else because it all seems stupid if I put it up against you and what I have to do for you. I can't audition for the school play or compete in the spelling bee or read a whole book cover to cover because I'm too busy thinking about you. And planning to run away to Vermont for you. And trying to figure out what makes you better and what's wrong and what it all means. I don't think about anything but you. Ever. Do you get that?"

It's then that I notice the shade of Danny's skin—an oceanic green.

"Stomachache?" I ask. Danny doesn't even fight back against my words, so I know it's a big sort of pain. A distracting, unbearable one. And I know if I step closer, the pain will ease up.

I take that step. Of course I do.

"It's bad," he says. He lowers his head, and I remember that this isn't what Danny chose. Neither of us chose this. I take another step to him and another.

Our knees touch and we sit in silence and Danny's hands move away from his sides and he relaxes. His normal Danny-color comes back. He isn't all better. If before he was the color of the ocean, now he's got a shade of sea glass in his cheeks and around his eyes. I think there's still a dull ache in his stomach.

But I'm making him better. I can feel it happening, like a light inside me. There's a thread between us, an invisible one, and when I'm near him, I can feel it waving. Then it stills.

It feels that simple. I sit and watch his body shift into something comfortable. It's as simple as a wrinkle in a bedsheet smoothing itself. I feel him unwrinkle, unwind, ease up.

"Have I always been able to do this?" I ask. "When we were little and you had poison ivy did yours get better when I put calamine lotion on your back? Did your broken foot heal fast because I was nearby?"

I wish my notebook were next to me and not in my desk

at home. There's still so much to research and learn and try to understand.

"I think you didn't start being able to help me until I needed you to," Danny says. "You know, like evolution. The need is there first, and then the solution appears, over time."

"Evolution?" We haven't gotten to evolution in science class yet. It's next, after we finish our unit on symbiosis.

"I read ahead. I know you like science, so I thought I'd try to understand some stuff too," Danny says, mumbling. He doesn't like admitting when he's being sweet, but he's being sweet.

I've been thinking I'm only ever doing things for Danny lately. But that's not true. It can't be. He does things for me all the time too, even if I don't know it.

"So the magic could disappear again, if you stop needing it," I say.

Danny shrugs. "I think so. But we won't need your magic soon. After Vermont. Right?"

"Right." In my head I think only *I hope I hope I hope* over and over.

I wonder if Rachel would agree with Danny's assessment. I think she probably would. *Magic comes and goes,* she said.

If I listen very, very closely, I can still hear the sounds of my birthday party next door. I wonder if they've saved a slice of cake for me. I wonder if it has a rose on it.

When Danny falls asleep, as he always eventually does, I sneak back home. I deserve a few moments of time that are about me before we leave tomorrow morning. I deserve a birthday, even if it's not the most important thing in the world right now.

"There you are!" Dad says when I'm back in the house. "I was getting worried you might not make it back." He knew without me telling him that if I wasn't in our house, I was at Danny's. That's how it's always been. No one has ever had to worry about where we are. We're almost certainly somewhere together.

Dad lights the candles and Elsa sings the loudest.

"I'm going to wish for Danny, too," she whispers before I close my eyes and blow out the candles. She gives Levi a look and he closes his eyes too, because three wishes are definitely better than one.

24

Dad leaves early in the morning, which means we need to get up even earlier in the morning.

I sneak downstairs and wait by the truck for Danny. I've packed peanut butter sandwiches and bags of Goldfish and pretzels and granola bars and everything else that I could get from my list, including my handmade trophy and Elsa and Levi's psychrometer, which they handed over at the party.

I pack it all in our Someday Suitcase.

Because I guess it's Someday.

When Danny arrives, he is already out of breath. Even his backpack stuffed with clothes and some of his teas and medicines seems too heavy for him.

"You need an inhaler," I say. Marco has asthma, so we all know about inhalers.

"I have you," Danny heaves. He grabs my arm. I hate the sound of his heavy breathing. The wheezing. The struggle.

"It's your breathing," I say. "We can't depend on me for that."

Danny grips my arm harder. We need to get into the truck soon. There's a little bed in the cab of the truck behind a curtain, and Dad probably won't open the curtain for hours and hours, so we'll be nice and hidden and cozy for a while.

Then I don't know. Hopefully we'll be too far into the trip for Dad to turn around and take us home.

Soon Danny and I are breathing in time with each other—big clear ins and outs. Then I can't hear his breathing at all—no rattle in his chest, no choke in his throat, just regular silent breathing.

"Wow," I say, because even if you know magic is there, it's still a surprise every time.

"Thank you," Danny says. I think it might be the first time he's thanked me for being magical. It feels good.

"We gotta get in," I say, and we climb into the sleeper. It's not a comfortable bed. It's tiny and hard, and the bumps in the road will make it impossible to sleep. But it's perfect for what we need to do.

"We're going to have to be quiet," I say.

"I know."

"Our parents are going to be worried," I say. "Really worried." My heart pounds. I like to be prepared. I like plans and lists and the scientific method. We don't have enough of that.

"I know," Danny says. I wait for him to come up with an idea for fixing their worry, a way to keep them calm. He doesn't.

My heart pounds harder and I keep looking through the window at my house. We wait for my dad to come outside, and for a moment I wonder if we should tell him what we're doing.

But if we tell him, he'll stop us from going. And we can't stop. Not now.

My dad leaves the house. He's got a thermos of coffee that I know my mom made and sweetened with cinnamon sugar for him, and he's frowning. I like to think he always looks this way when he leaves for a drive—like he's really sad to go.

"We can't worry about anything but getting there," Danny whispers. "Nothing else matters, as long as we get to the clinic. I'm feeling . . . I've been doing . . . when you're not around, I'm bad. I'm getting worse. You need to know I'm getting a lot worse. Every day I'm worse." Danny's voice chokes but not because of asthma or anything else.

"I didn't know—"

"I knew if I said I was worse you would find a way to never ever leave my side," Danny says. "I couldn't do that to you."

I shouldn't be shocked at the ways Danny takes care of me—they've always been there—but I'm shocked anyway. I'd been feeling angry and twisty and turny and topsy-turvy over having to take care of him and having to be near him and how badly he's been needing me. But all along he's been worried about me, too.

I take his hand.

This. This is why we are best, best, best symbiotic friends. This is why it's worth it to sneak away in my dad's truck and go to Vermont. This is why I'll do anything I can, anything at all, to fix him.

He squeezes my hand and we have to be quiet as mice as we drive through Florida and Georgia and the Carolinas.

Danny naps somewhere around South Carolina. It's hot back here and sticky, and Dad has been playing sports radio for hours and hours. They yell and scream, but at some point it starts to sound like a lullaby to Danny, I guess.

I don't sleep. I just watch Danny. I lay my hand on his forehead and focus on that feeling of being connected by a thread, of shifting something healthy in me into him.

It works.

If I could get my notebook out and write in it, I'd write down that it really, really works.

A PERFECT DAY WITH DANNY

Today is a perfect day.

We are huddled in the cab of Dad's truck, and it's hot and cramped and scary, but it's also wonderful.

"We've never done something like this before," Danny whispers. "This is our very first adventure."

It's true. Danny and I have done everything together our whole lives, but everything we have done has been predictable and safe and routine. It's been great, because we've been together, but we have spent all our days at the pool and in our backyards and stuffing our faces at the Sunday night cookouts and inventing games of tag with Jake and passing notes and games of Snowman back and forth during class.

We've been at the mall and the movies and sometimes some other kid's birthday party. But we haven't had a proper adventure.

"I'm not even thinking about getting in trouble," I say, which seems impossible because I love following the rules, but there's a buzz in my chest and my fingers seem to have a pulse. Sometime in between South Carolina and North Carolina, I stop being scared and start being thrilled.

The truck hiccups over speed bumps and potholes, and every time Danny and I crack up. We have to keep our laughter quiet, so we blow out our cheeks and turn red with the holding it in. Our eyes tear up from how badly we want to let the laughter out, and that only makes it funnier and better. We hide our faces in our elbow crooks, and kick each other when little giggles sputter out.

We count the bumps in the road and try to keep our bodies stiff and see who can stay the most upright every time the truck bounces. We make faces for the people talking on Dad's sports show—a silly frowny face for the man with the deep bellow, a fishy face for the man who talks very quickly, a crazed openmouthed smile for the woman who laughs at everything.

We snack on trail mix and Goldfish, and the further away we get from Florida, the further away I feel from everything that's happened over the last few weeks. Out on the road we are Danny and Clover again. We are wild, we are fearless, we are goofy and silly and funny. We are best, best friends who know how to stay laughing through all the bumps in the road.

I thought this was a road trip to get to Vermont to fix Danny, but it's fixing me, too. Danny is well for the whole ride. He doesn't cough or sniff or complain about earaches or stomachaches once, and I stop thinking of his sickness and everything I'm scared of.

For hours and hours, in the tiny bed with Danny, there's nothing to be scared of at all.

We're free.

I dream about snow and adventures and the long, long highway. I bet that's what Danny dreams about too.

We must sleep for a while, for longer than we should have, because at some point when my back is a little sore and my head is cloudy, I get woken up. By Dad.

"CLOVER?" he booms. His voice shakes the whole truck. His voice shakes *me*.

"Dad," I say, in my mouse voice. Danny keeps snoring.

"What in the WORLD are you doing back here?"

The darkness is lit up by lights on other trucks. We're at one of the truck stops Dad's told me about, and I guess I knew this would happen. When you don't have a plan, things can go wrong pretty quickly.

Even though Dad's face is twisty and strange, I'm still secretly excited about our trip and the sound of crickets and the chill in the air.

"Hi, Dad," I say. I want him to smile. I want him to see how good what we've done is.

I nudge Danny awake. We can explain better together.

Dad doesn't look mad, exactly. He looks scared and confused and amped up. He's breathing heavy and sweating. But his eyes have a squint that says he really wants to know if we're okay.

"We're okay," I say.

"Does Mom know you're here? It's been . . . you've been here since this morning? It's been hours and hours and hours, Clover. Your mother must be—Danny's mother must be—Mom said you were with your friend Elsa. What were you thinking? What possible reason could you have for being here? I've never seen anything like this from you before, Clover. Not anything! And *Danny*. You're a sick kid. You can't be in a truck miles away from your doctors. I can't believe either of you would be so—I have to call your parents—they must be worried sick—"

"I told them I'd be with Clover," Danny says. He shrugs. "They know when I'm with her—they know I'm safe."

Dad scrambles for his phone and he paces outside the

.ruck calling Mom and Danny's parents, waving his arms around, raising his voice on words like *completely unaware* and *what were they thinking* and *irresponsible* and *reckless* and *downright dangerous*.

"We are in so much trouble," I say.

"He'll still let us go to Vermont, right?" Danny looks out the window. There's nothing to see yet. Vermont is still far away.

"We're really far north," I say. "He can't turn around now. He has a very tight delivery schedule. Our plan will work." I feel a little guilty for how mad Dad is, but I'd feel even guiltier if I didn't do everything I could to help Danny.

Dad's hanging up his phone and heading back to the truck. He keeps shaking his head to himself. He flings the door open.

"I'm shocked," Dad says. "And hurt. We've trusted you, Clover. I'm disappointed, too. And scared. I thought I could depend on you. I need explanations. And apologies. And some honesty from both of you."

I'm shaky, but I know I need to explain everything to Dad anyway. "We needed to get to Vermont," I say.

"Is this about that clinic? Clover. You know Danny's parents are in charge of Danny's health care." Dad is still sort of shouting, but it doesn't sound the way it does when he's yelling at me about accidentally breaking his computer or being mean to Jake.

"They wouldn't let him go to Vermont," I say. "He's really sick, Dad. He's sick in the scary way. Like what Jake said. When we were making sundaes . . ." I look at Danny. He doesn't cringe from what I'm implying. He is steady and solid and okay, somehow. "I can't lose Danny," I whisper.

"We have to go back now. Look at all the time I've lost. Do you see how selfish this was? I could get in trouble at work. Your actions have consequences for other people, and I thought you were mature enough to know that." Dad isn't listening. He isn't hearing me at all. He doesn't hear how I'm hurt and desperate and also totally sure this is the only option.

"We can't go back," Danny says. He hasn't been saying anything at all, and I'm relieved to hear his voice, to let my own voice rest for a minute. If I talk any more right now I'm going to burst into desperate tears and Dad won't be able to hear me at all.

"That's not for you to—" Dad barely looks at Danny. At us. He looks at his phone and his watch and the road and the truck. He keeps shaking his head.

Danny takes a big breath. He looks at me, but I have no idea what he's going to say. We don't have a plan for this. I didn't think through everything the way a good scientist is supposed to. I didn't think about Dad's anger and disappointment. I'm losing hope.

"Sometimes late at night my parents think I'm sleeping, but I'm not. I hear the things they say." Danny looks at Dad to see if his posture or face have changed. Not yet. He is texting someone. He is scratching his head and sighing. It doesn't stop Danny. He goes on. "They're scared. My parents are scared and sometimes, late at night, they talk about what would happen if—if I can't get better. They don't know what else to do. The doctors are telling them to prepare. Do you know what that means? Prepare? I think I know. They're pretending it's okay, but when the whole world is dark and quiet, they admit that it's not. Even my parents are losing hope." Danny's voice doesn't shake, but my hands start to. And my knees. All this time I've been thinking I have secrets from Danny, but he's been keeping secrets from me too. He's been carrying burdens and sadnesses all by himself too.

Dad is finally listening.

"I need hope," Danny says.

I think we are all stunned into silence—me and Dad and Danny too. There are a bunch of other trucks around, music coming from some of them. A few men wander around and pat each other on the back, and there's a place to eat right ahead of us—it looks greasy and delicious. The sign is falling down, but I think it's meant to say *Frank's*.

It is the last place in the world I ever imagined having

a Serious Conversation. I can smell french fries and something bitter and unidentifiable and fumes from all the trucks. Dad looks comfortable here, and it's strange to see him in his other life, but a little nice too.

Dad stretches his neck, then his arms. He wipes his brow.

"I want you to have hope too," he says after a great long while. "Look. How are you feeling? Do we need to get you to a doctor? Your health is the number one priority."

Danny stands up like we're in the army all of a sudden. He has the straightest back and widest eyes.

"I feel great, sir," he says. He's never called my dad sir, not once, but today my dad is acting like someone who needs to be called sir.

"Great?" Dad says. He puts a hand on Danny's forehead. He looks perplexed. He hasn't seen Danny doing great in weeks and weeks.

"He's fine, Dad," I say. "He's good. When he's with me, he's good."

"That's not how Danny's sickness works, honey," Dad says.

"Yes, it is," I say. "Watch." I know now is the moment for us to tell my father. Danny told us what he needed to tell us, and now it's time to show Dad the other thing. The maybe magic.

I get out of the truck. Dad puts a hand on my shoulder.

"Where do you think you're going now?" he asks, and I see that it's going to be a long time before he trusts me the way he used to.

"Right over there," I say, pointing to a trash can a few yards away.

The thing between Danny and me has grown stronger and more vital in the past few days. I know if I'm even a little bit away from him, he'll start feeling sick again right away.

I think it means he's even sicker than before. It might mean I'm even more magical, too.

Dad eyes me suspiciously as I walk to the trash can, but I walk slowly so he knows I'm not trying anything tricky. I just need him to see. I need him to understand.

The stars are bright, wherever we are, so I look up at them while I wait to hear Danny cough or moan or sneeze. It's a risk, but it's the kind of risk we have to take now. It takes about a minute and a half.

Then:

"Oh my God! Oh my GOD, what's happening? Danny?? DANNY?"

I run back from the trash can. It's a short distance, but my dad's voice sounds so scared I can't run fast enough.

Danny is on the ground, trying to get a breath of air. His face is drained of color, and his eyes are closing.

"What happened?" Dad says. His ear is at Danny's chest; he's putting Danny's head in his lap.

"I've got it," I say, but I'm shaking. This is worse than what I'd imagined. I thought Danny would start feeling a little sicker. I thought it would be a slow transition. I figured there'd be some coughs or maybe he'd throw up and it would be gross, but we could prove something to my dad. I didn't know there'd be . . . this.

I try not to think about the conversations Helen and Ross have apparently been having late at night. I try not to think about how terrified Dad sounds and how many times Danny's been to the hospital.

I take a deep-down breath and take Dad's place, putting my knee under Danny's head and my hand on his forehead. I close my eyes. I try to hear his heartbeat and match it to mine.

Rachel says at some point you learn how to harness your magic, and I think that's what I'm doing now. At first the magic was mysterious and strange. Now it's a bit more like science.

Come back come back come back, I think in my head.

And for a few awful minutes, he doesn't. He wheezes and gasps, but I can tell real breath isn't getting into his lungs. He is grimacing like it hurts, and his eyes are closed.

"We need to call an ambulance," Dad says.

239

My heart pounds.

He is so much sicker than I want to believe. My stomach churns and my brain dizzies up and I know, now, why Ross and Helen are so scared.

I'm scared too.

I'm scared I'm losing Danny.

He stills.

I focus all my energy on him, all the magic and healing and symbiosis and best friendship. I focus all the hope in the world on him, because I know now that that's what he needs most of all.

His breaths start to come in deep and strong.

And his cheeks get pinker.

And I have fixed him, again.

Dad is stunned.

I'm a little stunned too.

Danny sits up. He rubs his eyes and stretches his neck. He looks at my dad.

"You have to take us to Vermont," he says.

26

Dad buys us sandwiches at Frank's that taste a little like plastic and salt and sleepiness. We sit outside the truck on the ground, under the stars, and talk about magic and science and the way friendship can grow into something life-changing and powerful and strange.

Mostly, though, we talk about hope. How badly we need it and how little of it other people have.

"I don't know about magic," Dad says.

"Me neither," I say, because I really don't know where science ends and magic begins, and which one we have.

Danny does something I've never seen him do before. He leans over, super close to Dad, and whispers into his ear, so quietly I can't hear a word.

Dad's face changes. It gets sad, and I catch the sadness before he remembers to turn it off and make his face normal again. He puts a big arm around Danny and squeezes.

"What'd you say?" I ask. Neither of them respond. "No secrets! What'd you say? We don't have secrets!"

Dad grimaces, and I think it's weird to keep seeing so many accidental expressions on his face. He looks down at his lap and Danny does too. I want to know what he said, but I also maybe don't want to know.

Whatever Danny said makes a difference. Dad softens. He reconsiders. He finishes off his sandwich and looks up at the stars.

"The Somerset Clinic, huh?" Dad says at last. He taps his fingers on his leg and jiggles his keys. He and Danny look at each other, both of them squinting, saying something without saying anything at all.

"It's still a long ways away," Dad says. "I have a few drops to make. You'll have to be patient."

"We don't mind," I say. "We're prepared."

Dad trills his lips. He jiggles his keys again. I can't figure out what he's thinking.

He nods once. He gets up and walks away with his phone. We can't hear the phone conversations he's definitely having with Mom and Helen and Ross, but we stay very quiet in case a word or two slips through.

When Dad is back by us, he looks up at the stars before speaking.

"Okay," he says. He clears his throat and it looks like it hurts. He looks like he's hurting.

I jump into my dad's arms to give him a grateful hug. He's strong and smells like chocolate and dust. I don't hug him nearly enough.

Dad's eyes look sad. "Looks like you two are going to see some snow after all," he says.

I feel Danny smile first.

Then I smile, imagining the way the flakes will float to the ground and make the world a brand-new, better place.

The ride is long. We stop a few more times, for food and rest and for Dad to make his deliveries. We stop at a motel where we eat a vending-machine meal of candy bars and chips and let Dad rest for a while. On the road, Dad says you don't have to worry so much about what time to eat lunch or dinner or what time to go to bed. You do what you need to do, when you need to do it. Danny loves this approach and calls it the best day of his life. I already had today on my List of Perfect Days, but I add a star next to the entry, so that I'll remember Danny agreed with me. Dad smiles, and I think he's happy he decided to let us keep going.

Sometime the next day, and we order milk shakes and

grilled cheese sandwiches. Dad's quiet and won't stop looking at Danny or checking his temperature with the palm of his hand. They keep giving each other secret looks, and I hate being on the outside of something.

"What'd you say to him?" I ask Danny when we're back in the truck and Dad's singing along with "Ramblin' Man."

"Don't worry about it," he says.

At another stop Dad makes us get out and stretch our legs and do jumping jacks. He says he's impressed by how little we're complaining while we move between the front seat with Dad and our familiar little bed when we get tired. He says it's nice to have some company on his long rides.

"I like knowing what you do," I say. "I like knowing what your days are like and the places you've been and what the truck feels like after a whole day of driving."

Dad smiles.

"You are one special kid, Miss Clover Jane," he says. He only ever uses my middle name when he's especially happy with me.

Danny does a few cartwheels, but he stays very, very close.

"Thank you," I whisper to my dad.

Dad nods, and watches Danny so hard I think his eyes don't even blink. We both do.

～∾

When we get very close to Vermont, Danny falls asleep in the bed and I sneak into the front with Dad. There isn't any snow yet, but I swear I can smell it, I can feel it on my skin. I'm colder than I've ever been, and Dad stopped right outside Boston to get Danny and me both parkas and thick socks and soft scarves. He promises that the second we get to Vermont we'll pick up hot chocolate, since there's absolutely nothing better in the world than hot chocolate on a cold day.

I have a fuzzy feeling in my belly and heart—sort of like excitement, but warmer and sweeter. It overrides the nervousness I feel at Dad and Danny's secret.

I zip up my parka.

"We're pretty close, Clo," Dad says. "You ready for all this? You really ready?"

I don't know what he means. I'm so focused on the snow and the cold I've forgotten about all the doctors and the clinic and what they might do to Danny. To me.

"I'm ready," I say.

"I hope it's what you want it to be, Clo," he says. "I also want you to be prepared that—"

I interrupt him. "You know why I like snow globes so much?" I ask. Dad looks confused; he's not used to me interrupting him. I usually hang on to his every word. He clears his throat. He scratches his chin. He looks at Danny again and again and again.

"Why's that, Clover Jane?" he asks.

We hit the *Welcome to Vermont* sign. It's green and declares Vermont the Green Mountain State. That seems all wrong, since the mountains are white tipped. I see them in the distance. Covered in what must be snow.

"They remind me that something is possible, even if it's not right in front of me, even if I've never seen it or can't even really fully imagine it. For a long time snow sounded like this magical, impossible thing. Then you got me that Pittsburgh snow globe and I shook it up and the snow fell over a regular sidewalk and a regular little house that looked a lot like our little house. And I got it. It existed, it was real, even if I didn't see it or understand it yet."

Dad looks at me for longer than he should, seeing as we're on the road.

"All this time, I thought the snow globes were sort of silly," Dad says with a chuckle.

"Not silly at all," I say, feeling like I'm entering a snow globe right here and now. "Hopeful."

"Hopeful's not silly at all," Dad says. And it's my very favorite thing he's ever, ever said.

I wake Danny up when we reach the white gates of the Somerset Clinic.

It looks the way it did on its website, but even better: a field of cows, a barn, a magnificent wooden building—a place that looks more like a home than a hospital. There are mountains in the near distance that the sun is starting to set behind, and an icy frost that makes the grass crunch under our feet.

But there isn't any snow.

"Hey," I say, flinging open the curtain separating the front of the truck from the back. "We're here." Danny is drowsy and confused. He rubs his eyes and looks out the window at the sign hanging off the gate.

"It's real," he says, like he wasn't so sure before.

"Of course it's real," I say.

"Will they let us in?" Danny asks.

"They have to."

Dad gets out of the truck first, and Danny and I follow behind. He leads the way inside the clinic. It smells nothing like hospitals smell. None of that plastic and rubbing alcohol smell. Instead I breathe in lilacs and chamomile tea.

There's a woman at the front desk. She has shiny hair and a thick blue scarf around her neck. She has a pen behind her ear and rosy cheeks and a serious mouth.

"Can I help you?" she says, and when she looks at us, I'm relieved to see she has kind eyes, too. Long eyelashes. The kind that would catch a lot of snow. Her sweater is red and cream and has a zigzag pattern and looks very Vermont-y. I want a sweater like that. I'd also like cheeks that are rosy from the wind and to be used to being cold inside and out.

Dad is the adult, so he should answer her, but I think he's suddenly realized he has no idea what the next step is. He drove us here. He forgave us. He bought us milk shakes and candy bars and mittens and hot chocolate. He listened to Danny's secret and got serious and sad. But now he's all out of things to do.

Danny is shaking next to me. I think it's fear this time, not sickness, but I take a step closer to him and put my hand on his elbow, just in case.

"We don't have an appointment," I say.

"Oh?" The woman with the shiny hair and scarf tilts her head.

"But we need to be here."

She looks back and forth between all of us. She settles on Danny.

"You're the one with the undiagnosed ailment?" she asks, even though she sounds pretty certain. Danny nods. Even his eyebrows are sweaty. It should be impossible, since I am goose bumped and shivering in here.

I like that she could tell just from looking at us. When she steps out from behind the front desk she's wearing sweater boots and is holding a notebook that looks a lot like mine. This makes me feel good, too.

"Usually we only take referrals," she says. "Do you have a referral?"

"Rachel Goldstein said we should come here," I say. "Does that count?"

"I don't think I know her," the shiny-haired woman says. "I'm Dr. Belinda Denn. And you are?"

"I'm Clover. This is Danny. And that's my dad."

"Harold," Dad says. I always forget he has a real name.

"How old are you, Danny?" Dr. Belinda Denn says. She holds out her hand to each of us, Danny last of all, and when he shakes it, I hope she feels the texture and temperature of

249

his skin, the boniness of his fingers, the way he is trembling a little, and weak.

"Ten," Danny says. I'd forgotten that I'm older than him for a few months of every year. Ten sounds so young, compared to eleven.

"And Harold here is your dad?"

"No. He's Clover's."

"I see. Hmm. Well, we'll need to talk to your parents. And we'll need to learn about what's troubling you. I'm going to want to talk to your old doctors. Then we can determine if you're a good fit." Dr. Belinda Denn finally takes out her notebook and my heart soars. I take out my notebook too. I've been carrying it in my backpack, keeping it close to me at all times, for exactly this moment.

"My parents will be here tomorrow," Danny says. I'm not looking forward to Helen and Ross joining us, but when Dad called to tell them what we'd done, they insisted. I don't know how he got them to agree with this, but I know it has something to do with what Danny whispered in his ear.

"You can talk to his doctors," I say, "but I've got everything you need to know right here. About Danny. And, well, about me too."

"About you too, hmm?" Dr. Belinda Denn says. I notice she has a snowflake necklace around her neck and a freckle on her nose. She takes my notebook.

"Danny's sick," I say. "But I make him better."

Dr. Belinda Denn gives me a long, intense look. Maybe at the clinic all they need to do is look at you, and they know everything about you. Maybe we'll leave here today with all the answers. Maybe we can tell Danny's parents not to come, we can drive the rest of Dad's trip with him and return home ready to swim and get sunburned and throw Jake in the pool with his floaties on and eat burgers outside with our families every Sunday forever and ever. Maybe. Maybe.

Or maybe not, a voice in my head that won't stop talking to me says. It is the same voice that keeps telling me the secret Danny told Dad is a bad one, a scary one, one I should be frightened of.

"I'll take this with me," Dr. Belinda Denn says, rubbing the soft cover of my notebook. "And we'll set you all up with rooms. And we'll see. We'll see what we can do."

I hear a cow mooing.

I smell apples baking.

I hear a few mechanical beeps that remind me we're in a medical place even if it doesn't seem like it.

I see a sick man in a wheelchair with tubes coming out of him.

"Hate to see the young ones," the man in the wheelchair says to Dr. Belinda Denn like we can't hear him.

I have no idea what to think about this place, except it's better than the hospital with its wiggly Jell-O and metal cots.

"Danny and I need the same room," I tell Dr. Belinda Denn. "We have to stay close."

~e

The rooms are beautiful, with big soft beds and red-checked curtains and cozy tan rugs that feel good against our feet. "Handmade," Dr. Belinda Denn said.

"I'm sleepy," Danny says. His eyes look like they're having trouble staying open, but he already slept so much, it doesn't make sense.

"You should be awake," I say, a little too forcefully. "You slept a lot. It's still pretty early. I'm right here. Don't you feel good?"

Danny shrugs.

I don't like when Danny shrugs.

"Are you excited?"

Danny shrugs.

"We're in Vermont! Stop shrugging! We did exactly what we said we'd do!" It's too dark to really make out the mountains, so I beg the sky to snow.

Snow will make Danny stop shrugging.

But it doesn't snow.

28

By the next day, Helen and Ross have their own room at the Somerset Clinic. They give Danny the world's biggest hugs and tell me what a great friend I am. I think they like the chill in the air and the unlimited supply of hot chocolate, but mostly they like being near Danny.

Dad has to go back on the road when they arrive. He gives me a stubbly kiss.

"I'll only be a few hours away if you need me," he says.

"I think this is going to work," I say. Dad's forehead creases. "Don't you?"

"I have hope," he says. He pauses, like he's not sure if he should keep going. Usually my parents know exactly what to do for all my different moods. They respond right away when I need something or ask about something or am freaking out about something. I don't like how unsure Dad looks. It's all wrong.

"What did Danny whisper to you?" I ask. "Why did you end up letting us come here?"

Dad shakes his head. He tears up a little. "I wish he wasn't so sick, Clover," he says. "But he is. And I hope he gets better. But he might not."

I think I feel my heart fall.

I think I feel the floor and the ceiling and the walls fall too. Vermont feels even colder, from those words.

"What did he say to you?" I ask again. But Dad won't tell me.

"The way you hope and believe in magic and believe in love is the most beautiful thing in the world," Dad says. "And nothing can take that away from you, okay? That's you. That's who you are. That's what got you here."

I nod, and I don't know exactly what he means, but I'm pretty sure it means that he believes in me. And that feels better than the Vermont chill or being on the highway or drinking hot chocolate on a cold day.

~~~

Danny has a million appointments over the next couple of days.

There are blood tests. And ear tests and nose tests and lots of lung tests. They test all his organs, and I can tell from their faces that they aren't so happy with what they're seeing.

"Your whole body is tired from trying to fight off different infections," one doctor says. "It's having trouble doing its job."

"You're going to get better," I say to Danny when we walk back to our room so the doctors can talk to Helen and Ross alone on our second day here. Danny tries to smile, but it doesn't look like one of his regular smiles.

That night, Danny falls asleep before me, and I whisper, "Please don't give up" before I fall asleep too. He doesn't respond, because he's sleeping, and I hate the silence that follows.

The next day they take more blood and do X-rays. They look inside his stomach and ask him a thousand questions about every time he's ever been sick.

"We know some of the things that are wrong," the doctor says. "But we don't quite know why yet."

At the Somerset Clinic, doctors talk in low voices and then say things very clearly. They talk right to Danny instead of just his parents the way other doctors sometimes do. I like the doctors here, even though I don't like what they're saying.

It doesn't snow, and when I go outside to check early on our fourth day at the clinic, Danny faints in the three minutes I'm not right next to him.

"I'm getting worse," he says when they rush me back inside to hold his hand and make him better. I close my eyes and feel our hearts and breaths connect and the thread between us goes taut and I fix him again.

I am officially scared, though.

I can't go to the bathroom without worrying Danny will get sicker.

I can't go for a walk or spend a night alone or read at one table while Danny reads at another.

Danny is right. He's getting worse. And the worse he gets, the closer I have to be, the less time I can spend away, until even a few feet of space and a few moments of time apart is too much.

"This is too much," Danny says.

"It's okay, it's okay," I say, but I want to walk in the brisk Vermont air and talk to a cow by myself. I want to drink hot chocolate on the porch of the clinic and watch the sun set over the mountains without Danny gripping my arm or pressing his knee against mine.

I wonder if the shrimp and the eels ever feel this way.

I wonder if they feel tired by how they have to work

together, how close they have to be. When I first saw that shrimp in that eel's mouth, it was beautiful, but now when I think of it I can feel how trapped it must feel, and how choked the eel must feel.

I would call Mom or Dad and tell them how I feel, or pull Dr. Belinda Denn aside to tell her how tired I am, but I can't, because Danny is always there.

On the fifth day, Danny and I sit next to each other on the doctor's table. It isn't really big enough for both of us, but it's safest this way.

"Do you know what autoimmune disorder means?" Dr. Belinda Denn says.

"Yes!" Danny says. "Well, no. Sort of. But I know my grandfather had one."

"That's right," Dr. Belinda Denn says.

I think about my notebook. I wrote *autoimmune disorder and Danny's grandfather* in it on my hypothesis page after he told me about it before. I scribbled a whole bunch of question marks and looked up what *autoimmune* meant. I'm a good memorizer—Ms. Mendez says famous scientists often have minds that remember facts well—and I recall it meant that the body was hurting itself.

I shiver.

"What Danny has is called common variable immune

deficiency. CVID. It's an immune deficiency that in Danny's case has left him vulnerable to other problems, like autoimmune manifestations and some complicated infections, lung disease, and anemia." I write all the words down in a new notebook now that Dr. Denn has mine, but the words are long and unfamiliar and frightening. "We believe your grandfather had something similar. We've seen many different kinds of autoimmune diseases here at the clinic."

Something in Danny relaxes. I don't feel any better, but I guess Danny does.

"It has a name," he sighs, like that's the only reason we came here. To name this thing that's eating him up. I want more than a name. I want to fix it.

"What about me?" I ask.

Dr. Belinda Denn smiles.

"You are perfectly healthy, Clover," she says.

"Well, right," I say, scooting a little closer to Danny. "But how am I fixing him?"

Dr. Belinda Denn smooths her already smooth hair.

"I know this is hard to understand," she says, "but not everything has an easy explanation. I think it has something to do with love and something to do with comfort and something to do with . . . well . . . I don't know the word for it, but the unexplained. Here at the Somerset Clinic, we try to look at people as whole people, not just little hurting parts of them. And you are two people with something very special and unexplained between you."

"The unexplained?" I ask. The Somerset Clinic is supposed to be a place for science and answers. It's supposed to be the place where they give Danny's illness a name and find him a cure. A real cure that isn't me. Danny scoots closer to me, but there's barely room between us to begin with.

Dr. Belinda Denn lowers her voice. "You've done wonderful, wonderful work in helping us figure out what's wrong with Danny, Clover. Your notes were instrumental in giving us all this information. But we're still figuring it out too. And some things can't be figured out so easily. So yes. What you have for Danny is beautiful and love-filled and special and a little scary. And unexplained."

Dr. Belinda Denn moves on to talk about treatments that they will try here at the clinic, like infusing his blood with healthy things and treating his other infections with antibiotics and steroids and some experimental treatments that I write down as best I can.

"We're going to do everything we can," Dr. Belinda Denn says. "But some of Danny's secondary issues are quite serious. His lungs and some of his organs aren't—in the place we want them to be."

I try to unhear the last thing she said.

I focus on the unexplained, the special, impossible, powerful thing between us.

Magic, I think, and I'm positive I can feel it shimmering and glittering and fluttering inside me. Magic. I hold on to it as tightly as I can.

29

Danny and I wait for it to snow the next morning.

We don't talk about CVID or what it means that they don't know how to fix it. We don't talk about how much worse he's feeling every day. Every hour. We don't talk about his grandfather or anything in my notebook.

We wait.

We are waiting for a lot of things: answers, healing, my dad to come back, another doctor's appointment for Danny, a time when we won't have to be within one foot of each other for Danny to be okay.

But right now, we are mostly waiting for snow.

We sit on the front porch of the clinic. There's a swing

there, a wooden one that squeaks when it goes back and groans when it goes forward and is just high enough that our legs don't touch the ground when we're in it.

"Do you think it will happen today?" I ask.

"The weatherman said it would," Danny says. The weatherman's name is Dale, and he has become our best friend here in Vermont. He wears plaid ties and has staticky hair. He pronounces the ends of his words very hard, like a door slamming, and I think this makes us trust him more.

The air is biting, but I have no idea if that's how it feels before it snows. I watch the mountains and wonder if they have answers. They are so tall and solid and beautiful that they must.

"How are you feeling today?" I ask. We have thermoses of hot chocolate and bellies full of pancakes and eggs with Vermont cheddar, so I feel great, but it's hard to tell with Danny.

"Okay," he says. I don't believe him. I move closer to him. He sighs. "It's not working as well anymore."

"I'm sorry." I don't know what else to say.

"It's not your fault. It's still better when you're here. But better isn't very good anymore."

His arms are even skinnier than usual, which is really saying something. Even his chin looks skinny. His throat. His nose. They have been filling us up with delicious food and hot drinks and covering us in the softest blankets. Those things fix me, they make me feel better. But they're not fixing what's wrong with Danny.

"They're going to figure it out," I say.

Danny shrugs.

"You're not the cure," he says at last, looking out at the not-snow.

"But I am!" I say. "That's what they said! They said they agree with me!"

"No," Danny says. "I'm getting sicker anyway." He takes this breath, this huge, huge breath, that's so big it feels like it might not even leave any air for the rest of us. "It's okay, Clover."

"It's not okay!" I say. "I'm not trying hard enough! I keep getting tired, but if I try harder, the magic will work and you'll be fine!" I'm crying, and I didn't even realize it. I don't know when it started, and I especially don't know when it will stop.

"Our friendship is so powerful it helped make me feel better. That's—I mean, how great is that? We have a magical friendship." Danny isn't crying. He actually looks okay, a fact I can't believe.

"Love with a twist," I say like a mantra.

Danny gives me a Danny smile. "They showed me other cases of people with CVID who got diagnosed here. And none of those people had someone like you. I'm so *lucky*, Clo. I get this terrible, mysterious, awful illness, but I'm still so lucky."

"How is that lucky?" I ask. The tears won't stop coming.

"You're what makes it lucky. I got a magical elixir in the form of my best friend. I got to realize how special you are and how huge our friendship is. I got to come on an adventure with you. I don't know. Now we're going to see snow. That's . . . that's everything I could want."

"But the snow's not even coming," I say through sniffs and sobs. "I'm supposed to be fixing you. We're supposed to have our perfect symbiosis!"

Danny laughs.

It is unexpected and true.

"You can't fix this, Clover," he says. "You're going to make such a good scientist. You really are. But Ms. Mendez says being a good scientist isn't about trying to change the world, it's about trying to understand the world."

I didn't know Danny ever listened in science class.

He rubs my shoulder, comforting me. It's been a while since it's been Danny comforting me, not the other way around, and I lean into his hand. I let him comfort me and I hang on to the way it feels.

"It'll come," Danny says, cool as a cucumber, sipping the world's most perfect hot chocolate on the world's squeakiest porch swing. "The snow will come."

It doesn't come. We don't move. I try to let go of all the worry and focus on the cold and the wet air. I imagine my worry as a heavy rope I've been pulling on for months, and my arms are tired and I'm sweating and the force on the other side has gotten stronger and stronger. I imagine letting go. I imagine my arms relaxing and finally being able to rest, no longer pulling so hard on that worry rope day after day after day.

I do it. Sort of. I let go. As much as I can.

Eventually Danny says, "Remember that day at the aquarium?"

I nod. Tears are frozen on my cheeks from earlier. I can feel them stuck there. I should add that day to my list of perfect days too.

"That was a great day," Danny says. "I thought you were so lame for liking science. And symbiosis. And then I saw it. We're like those fish."

"Exactly," I say. "And if something happens to you, I can't survive. Like the fish."

"Even if something happened to me," Danny says, finally, finally looking right at me and not at the place where snow should be, "the love stays forever. Love is what makes us symbiotic. And that's never going anywhere. Even if something happens to me. Okay? You hear me?"

"The love remains," I say, trying to sound as calm and okay as Danny. Maybe he's right. Rachel says magic comes and goes, and mine is getting weaker, but love is always there. If magic is love with a twist, and the magic goes . . .

Love remains.

30

It doesn't snow, but everyone is bundled up at the clinic and there's a fire in the fireplace in the lounge and Danny and I play checkers and don't have to get any blood drawn. We haven't spent much time in the lounge, but other patients are here all the time, in flannel robes and thick sweaters and handmade scarves. We say hi to a few of them.

There's one woman in long pajamas and a woolly striped scarf and super-soft slippers who introduces herself to us. Her name is Isabelle. Isabelle introduces us to Glen, who wears a huge sweatshirt three sizes too big and a smile that's a few sizes too big for his face, too.

"Best friends," Isabelle says. Danny and I are on the

cozy gray carpet in front of the fireplace, and Isabelle and Glen flank us on either side in checkered armchairs. I can tell they've been at the clinic a long time.

"Us?" I ask.

"Of course you!" Glen says. "Look at you! The best of friends. Clearly."

"True," I say.

"Only when she's not annoying me," Danny says, and I love him a little more than the second before, because Danny will tease me anytime, anywhere.

"He's the annoying one," I say.

"They sounds like us sixty years ago," Glen says.

"They sure do," Isabelle says.

"You guys are best friends too?" I ask. Checkers is boring and I like the way the fire sounds when it crackles and the warmth on my cheek that is facing it. This is exactly what I thought of when I thought of Vermont, except with snow. If this were a snow globe, we'd be in a tiny cottage lit up from inside with orange light, and with enough shaking we'd be in a glittery snowstorm.

But it's not a snow globe, so it's gray and still outside the huge picture windows.

"Lifetime best friends," Glen says, leaning back in his armchair. I can hear his bones crack. "And married."

"Ew," Danny says. "That would never happen with us."

"*Never*," I say with a grin.

Glen and Isabelle laugh.

"What are you two in for?" Isabelle asks.

"Common variable immune deficiency," Danny says, but he sounds a little proud. He's happy it finally has a name, even if the name is a scary one.

"Impressive," Isabelle says. "They haven't quite figured us out yet. Magical place, huh?"

Danny and I exchange a look and nod.

Then Danny coughs and his face goes white.

The cough makes my heart hurt and my eyes water. I touch his knee, and the cough relaxes a little but doesn't stop. A week ago it would have been all gone. His cheeks get rosy again, right away, like little stoplights lighting up out of nowhere.

"Well, look at that," Glen says. "You see that, Isabelle?"

"I sure did," Isabelle says. She shakes her head like she can't believe it. "I've never seen something so beautiful in all my years."

I guess she's talking about me and Danny and the magic between us. I didn't know how visible it had become, how powerful and obvious. I blush. Danny blushes.

"Never seen anything like it," Glen says.

"Guess you've never been to the aquarium," Danny says. I keep my hand on his knee and laugh. He laughs too—a big, boisterous laugh with only a few little coughs in between.

It feels good.

I wish his cough would stop.

I wish it would snow.

The fire keeps crackling.

Danny and I go to sleep in our twin beds. Right before I fall asleep, he whispers, "Dale said it's going to snow late tonight. Let's stay up."

"I'm so tired. And Dale is always wrong about snow," I say. I waited all day today for snow and nothing happened. Now I'm sleepy from the fire and the cold and the promise of more tests and research and reading tomorrow. They found out that not only did Danny's grandfather have CVID, but his great-grandfather and great-great-grandmother did too.

"A fascinating and unusual family disease," a doctor who was not Dr. Belinda Denn said.

"I wish your CVID didn't have so many complications,

Danny," Dr. Belinda Denn said. She looked worried.

All that talk about Danny's illness wore me out. I can't wait for snow that won't ever come. I'm already half dreaming about Jake and me traveling down a river on an alligator and Elsa singing Christmas carols.

"I'm staying up," Danny whispers. His bed is close to the window, so he doesn't have to go anywhere. He seems to be feeling okay, with my bed one foot away and both of us breathing the same chilly air.

"Clover?" Danny says, interrupting my dream beginnings.

"Mmmm?"

"Dr. Belinda Denn admitted you're magical today. I wasn't going to tell you. I don't want you getting a big head. But she said she couldn't think of another explanation. She said it when no one else was around. But she said it. Pretty cool, right?"

I smile in my sleep.

A real live doctor said magic is real. My magic is real.

"Pretty cool, Danny," I mumble, and my dream shifts into a Sunday cookout with Danny and our families and Jake all dressed up in a tux, tap dancing.

～e～

"Clover?" I shift. I hate waking up. "Clover?" My eyes hurt and I don't want to open them. My head is fuzzy and heavy. "Clover, you have to get up."

My dad's voice is thick and strange and all wrong because Dad isn't the one sharing this room with me, Danny is.

"You're here?" I ask, trying to understand the awake world while I leave the dream one behind. It's cold. I pull up my quilt.

"I'm here," Dad says. "I got back late. It's still late."

I look around. It's dark.

Danny's not here.

Danny's not here, next to me.

"Where's Danny???" I say, popping up in bed, fully awake. Dad puts one of his big hands on my shoulder. It's something I've been doing to Danny a lot, something he's been doing to me, too. We've been grabbing each other, trying to suck as much magic as possible out of each moment.

This is different.

There's no magic between Dad and me.

"Where is he???" I ask again. There's lightning and thunder in my chest, and I'm so dizzy I don't think I can stand up.

"Clover," Dad says, and I hate the way he says my name. Like he's sorry.

"WHERE?"

"He's gone, honey." Dad clears his throat. I don't understand. I do, but I don't.

"Gone where?"

Dad rubs his own eyes and looks out the window. I wonder if it snowed.

Then I don't care.

I grip the edge of my bed, but it doesn't help anything. Dad takes my other shoulder so he's holding both sides of me. His face is all wrong.

"Danny died," he says.

It is the most anything has ever hurt. More than a sunburn or stubbed toe or being called ugly by mean neighborhood boys or getting food poisoning from one of my mom's meals or Jake pinching me or biting me or slapping me across the middle.

And with the hurt there's confusion. It doesn't make sense, like a sentence with a missing noun. The whole world is a sentence with a missing noun.

But mostly there's hurt.

"Noooooo," someone wails, and I guess that someone is me.

"I'm so sorry, Clover. I'm so, so sorry," Dad says, but the words don't mean anything at all. I look around the room like it's a joke, like Danny's here. He isn't.

"I was right here! How could he? When I was HERE? I was fixing him! Dad, no. NO." My hands are shaking and my heart and voice too. All of me.

"He snuck outside," Dad says. "It snowed a little and he wanted to see. And he did see. Glen and Isabelle, two of the patients, saw him. They watched the snow fall with him."

"Why would he do that? He knew he needed me. I would have gotten up. I would have held his hand and watched the snow with him! I would have done anything!" I'm crying so hard now that I can barely breathe, so Dad rubs my back and doesn't answer my questions. He says *shh, shh, shh* like an ocean, and I try to get lost in the sound because everything else is unbearable.

"He wasn't getting better, honey," Dad says. "He knew he wasn't getting better. That's what he whispered to me. He told me he knew he wasn't going to make it. He knew he was too sick. But he wanted to have a last adventure with you. He knew, Clover. He knew it was time to let go."

He told me to let go too, and I did. He told me to let go of that rope of worry and I tried to do just that, but I didn't know what he meant.

Or I did know, but I couldn't hear it quite right. I pretended not to know.

I shake my head and bury it under the blankets and try to find a world under there where Danny's fine and it's six months ago and none of this has happened and everything's okay.

~⁓~

I have so much inside me and nowhere to put it. I am a crowded dresser with clothes hanging out and the drawers won't close and it's messy and ugly and overflowing.

I'm also an empty room.

I am nothing and everything and I am not myself because I can't be Clover without Danny.

⁓

Everyone tries to talk to me on my way out, but I don't want to talk to anyone. And when we get to the porch, I see there's no snow.

"I thought you said he watched the snow," I say to Glen and Isabelle, who hold hands and frown and watch me leave.

"He did," Glen says. "He loved it. He said you'd love it too. He was happy it would be here waiting for you in the morning, he said." Glen gives me a mug of hot chocolate and an apple cider doughnut, something I've only heard of here in Vermont, and I think of how much Danny liked hot chocolate and apple cider doughnuts these last few days.

"Where is it?" I ask. "Where's the snow?" My voice is all broken and soft and not mine.

"It melted," Isabelle says.

I'd forgotten, I guess, that snow melts.

In my snow globes, it's always there, ready to be shaken up and swirled again.

List of Things I Don't Want to Do by Myself, Without Danny

- Go to the pool
- Eat ice cream
- Eat sandwiches
- Eat
- Go to the mall
- Sing
- Work on science projects
- Ask questions
- Answer questions
- Run away
- Stay home
- Dream
- Sleep
- Wake
- Listen to "Ramblin' Man"
- Laugh at my problems
- Play tag
- Stand still
- I can't think of a single thing I want to do without Danny.

32

There is a funeral when I'm back in Florida. There are flowers and songs and memories of Danny.

Some of them make me smile.

Some of them make me cry.

There is a letter from Dr. Belinda Denn. She uses the word *magic* and tells me she's never seen anything like it. I don't know if it helps, exactly, but I keep the letter.

There is a card from Rachel, who says magic doesn't last forever, but love does. I think about telling her Danny and I already figured that out together, but I get too sad when I write down Danny's name.

There's a teddy bear from Jake that I love more than I

ever thought I could love a stuffed animal, and a Vermont snow globe from Dad.

"I didn't know if this would make you sad or happy," he says. It's a snow globe exactly like the one I had in my head the day we played checkers with Glen and Isabelle. A wood cabin with an orange fire inside, making the outside glow a little. There are pine trees and a pair of skis leaning against the outside of the cabin.

I wish Danny and I could have learned how to ski.

I shake it. Snow gusts around, circling in on itself until it settles. I imagine Danny watching the snow fall. I wonder what he thought of it. I wonder if he touched it. I wonder if it had a sound when it touched the ground. I wonder if it was everything we thought it would be.

Or more. I hope it was even more.

I think it's going to make me sad, but it makes me a little happy.

"I love it," I say.

Other people bring me snow globes too. Brandy brings one with cats in the snow and Marco brings one with New York City in the snow and Ms. Mendez sends one of a forest with fairies in the snow. I think it's her way of telling me she believes in magic, too.

Ms. Fitch sends me something extra special with her snow globe. It's the outline of me, filled in by everyone in class. Inside the me-outline are hearts and stars and glitter and snowflakes and words that I guess people associate with me. *Kind, fun, smart, sweet, good friend.* In the center of the glittery heart that Elsa drew on my outline, Ms. Fitch has drawn a picture of Danny with his spiky hair and squinty eyes and easy smile.

I was worried I'd stay empty forever.

I hang the outline on my wall right away and watch it, looking for hope.

~e

Elsa brings me a snow globe a week after the funeral.

"Maybe I could sleep over," she says. She tried telling me how the science fair went, but I didn't want to hear about it. She tried to tell me what she remembered about Danny, but I didn't want to hear that either. All I want to do is look at snow. We watch as the ice-skating rink in the globe she brought me gets doused in snow. A little blond girl with pigtails and a pink hat has one leg in the air and the other on the ice. I wish Danny and I had learned how to skate.

"I don't think it's a good idea," I say, which is what my mother says when she's saying no to a sleepover, and it usually makes me stop asking.

"Maybe you don't want to be alone," Elsa says. Her nose is tilted up in a way I'd never noticed before.

I think she might be right, but I also think I mostly just want Danny here.

Something inside me is wrong. I feel like my heart has a fever. Like it's sweating and shivering and dreaming crazy dreams. Like it has that awful, sensitive, untouchable feeling that my skin got last time I was sick. Danny used to call the feeling the Terrible Tingles. My heart has the Terrible Tingles and is in a panic.

"Are you okay?" Elsa says. She puts her hand on my knee, and it reminds me of the million times I did that to Danny. It doesn't magically make me feel better because not everything can be magic. But I let her keep it there and it's okay. It's nice, knowing she's there.

Not magical. But nice.

We stay quiet. Elsa picks up the snow globes everyone's given me one by one and makes them all snow. There are more than twenty of them to add to my collection, which already has thirty. I watch them swirl and I miss Danny.

But I also think for one second that other people, not just Danny, know a little bit about what I need and what I like. Seeing the snow globes as Elsa furiously shakes them up, trying to keep them all snowing before they settle, is pretty amazing, actually. I loved Danny most of all, but there are a lot of other people who love me too, I guess.

I think I even smile. Not for long, but for a moment.

"Can I draw?" Elsa says, and I give her paper and a pencil. I'm glad she's not making me do anything. Not even making me talk. I lie on my back and stare at the ceiling and miss my best friend.

We stay like that for a while and I listen to Elsa's pencil on paper. It's a nice sound. I breathe in time with it. It calms me down a little. It must be the sound Ms. Fitch's pencil made when she drew Danny into my outline.

I think about the self-portraits we drew in art class, too, and how Danny is in mine and looks like a ghost, in the background. The thought collapses me, and I don't cry, but I hang my head and tell Elsa to go.

She does, but not before leaving behind her drawing.

"You told me about when you and Danny were little," she says. I'm immediately mad I told her any of me and Danny's history. It's ours. I have to protect it with my life. It's all I have left. "You and your dads going down to the water in the mornings when you were babies, to watch the sunrise. Your dads eating bacon while you guys gurgled and napped and nuzzled. That's a nice memory."

I wince at the word *memory*. I don't think I want to hear that word ever again.

I don't reply. The drawing is in my lap anyway, and long after Elsa leaves I finally look at it. It's me and Danny, all grown up, watching the sun come up. There aren't any details. It's just me and Danny and the sun and nothing else, not even grass or water or bacon.

It's good, of course. Elsa's always good at art.

I feel a little less alone, looking at it, especially next to all the snow globes and the outline from Ms. Fitch. There's magic in the picture, in all the gifts I've been given, and I feel a tiny hint of the connection to Danny. The warmth. The love with a twist.

I feel some warmth for Elsa too. I don't think Danny would mind.

I'm not saving him; it's too late for that. But it was never about the saving. It was about who we could be together. And hope. And friendship. And love, love, love.

The picture doesn't get all of that, but there's something there to hold on to.

⁓

A few hours after Elsa leaves, I join Mom and Dad and Jake for dinner. They look extra excited to see me at the table, because I haven't been wanting to eat dinner with the family since I got back from Vermont.

There's a place set for me anyway, even though they weren't sure I'd come, and I love that it's all set, waiting for me, like I'm there even when I'm not there.

Dad made tacos, and everyone watches while I scoop meat and cheese and avocados onto my tortilla. "Where are the best tacos in the world?" I ask, just to fill up the silence of them watching me and waiting for me to cry some more.

"Mexico, I'd guess," Dad says.

"Mexico's close," I say.

"Are you going on another adventure?" Jake asks, like now that I've been to Vermont I might become a cool traveling jet-setter.

Sometimes I think Jake's not paying much attention to everything going on in my life, but people are wrong about Jake all the time, so maybe I'm wrong about that, too.

I don't answer, because the answer—*I can't go without Danny*—will make me cry, and I don't want to cry. But Mom answers for me.

"Clover is going to go on so many more adventures," she says.

I don't agree or disagree, I just polish off a couple of tacos and listen to Jake ask about where different countries are. But when I'm back in my room and trying to get to sleep, I can't stop thinking about what Mom said and how close Mexico is and that it would be cool to go there and eat the world's greatest tacos, if only I could take Danny with me.

I wander out of bed and go to the Someday Suitcase. Mom unpacked it for me, because I thought it would be too sad to take my winter clothes out and put them in the back of the closet, never to be worn again.

I couldn't go anywhere without Danny right now. I don't even want to go to school without Danny, let alone on an adventure. But the Someday Suitcase isn't for what you're ready for right now. It's for what you may want to do later. It's for Someday.

I let myself make a list. I haven't made a list since Vermont, and I don't write it down, but I keep it in my head. It's a list of places I may want to go. Mexico and the Grand Canyon and Paris and New York City.

The list makes me smile, but it makes me sad, too, because Danny won't get to go to those places with me.

I get up to go back to bed, but before I do, I find the picture Elsa drew. I fold it very, very carefully and pack it into the top pocket of the suitcase.

If I'm going to go on adventures someday, I'll need to have a little bit of Danny with me.

He was the adventurous one, after all. Danny was good at crazy ideas, and I was good at finding ways to make them come true. Now I'm going to have to do both.

I zip the Someday Suitcase back up, with Elsa's picture of Danny inside, waiting for me, whenever I'm ready.

33

Birds get hurt more often than you'd think.

Unless you're looking for them, you don't always see them. But once your eyes are open, they're there. Here. Everywhere. Limping and struggling and sometimes dead. They fly into our huge picture windows and something about that is ridiculously sad to me.

I watch them for weeks.

I watch them before school and after school and when I'm supposed to be doing homework or trying to have other friends. It's hard to have other friends.

I find a hurt bird on the lawn two weeks after Danny's funeral, and it's painful to see it trying to fly, I'm not sure

I can stand it. It does these little jumps, effortful and melancholy, but its wing won't flap. Its body won't lift. Its little bird self refuses to soar.

I haven't been able to fix anyone or anything since Danny died. Mom got a cold and I tried to fix it. Jake sprained his ankle and I tried to fix that too. It didn't work.

But I feel a pulse of something, upon seeing the broken bird.

"Heyyyy," I say, waving at it like it's a new kid at school and I'm trying to be friendly. The bird doesn't wave back, because it's a bird.

I've got a huge peanut butter and banana sandwich and a picnic blanket, and I'm missing the way it felt to have magic. I drop some banana on the ground and wonder if the bird will join me. If we could have lunch together, the bird and I. It's hard being around my human friends right now, but a bird sounds about right.

The bird doesn't even notice. I inch closer.

I don't know if it's the missing Danny that does it or the being near the bird, but I feel a rush of the thing I used to feel when I was near my sick best friend. Connection, or something like it. Warmth. Generosity. Hope. Claustrophobia.

Magic.

My magic.

I can fix the bird. I'm sure of it.

I get as close to the bird as I can without touching it. I'm afraid to touch it. Its wings look dirty and have a sheen of oil on them. And I've heard years of stories about baby birds who are forever infected by human smell when a human touches them. Birds whose mothers won't ever return to them. Birds who have been given up on.

I'm not sure if this is a baby bird or an adult bird, but I don't want it to become one of *those* birds. The ones who won't ever have families again. Who will die anyway, from loneliness or heartbreak or not knowing how to take care of themselves.

I put a finger so close to the bird that it almost touches.

And I wait for it to matter. I wait for my magic.

The bird hops and jumps and its little bird wings flutter but don't spread out, don't catch the wind and lift it up. I bring my face close to the bird's face, not sure what I'll find there. I've never been a huge animal lover. I like them and all, but I don't feel drawn to them the way Jake does. Jake can have a whole conversation with a dog. We take him to the zoo when he's having a particularly bad day, and he stares at the giraffes and pandas like he's seeing them brand-new every time. He bows his head. He grins at the monkeys and tries to climb in with the lions.

"They'll hurt you!" Mom said the last time he tried that.

"No," Jake said, calm for the first time in weeks. "I

know how they're feeling. They won't mind as long as I don't hurt them." I believed him, too.

That's not how I am around animals. I feel awkward, like I'm doing it wrong and they know I'm not an animal person. But I lean in to the bird anyway, and its beak is so sharp it astonishes me.

I feed the bird a little bread from my sandwich. It pecks at the ground, wanting more and more. I close my eyes and wait for the feeling to come, the connection between us to be made. I wait to cure the little bird like I always cured Danny.

It doesn't come, exactly, but after a long time on the lawn, the bird and I sharing space but not much else, it lifts off.

It floats in the air a little, and I'm terrified it won't stay up, but it flaps its wings harder and harder and soon it's in the treetops, looking down at me.

I don't think it's cured, but it's found a new way to fly.

"I did that, right?" I whisper into the air, and pretend Danny's beside me.

And for a moment, for the best moment, I feel almost like he is.

A PERFECT DAY
WITHOUT DANNY

I ask it not to, but time moves forward anyway.

Elsa comes over once a week during December and January.

"You should come to Levi's after school," she says in February, the day before winter break. I'm not sure it's a good idea. I've been having a sad day. They hit sometimes, out of nowhere, and hold me down, make it hard for me to do things.

I shrug. I know a good day will come again, but not today.

The best days are the ones where I think about all the happy memories with Danny and the happiness is still there.

The happiness isn't gone, the magic's not gone, so Danny's not all the way gone either.

Love remains.

"Will you please come to Levi's?" Elsa asks again. She doesn't give up on anything, and I know she'll keep asking me until I say yes. Even though I'm having a sad day, I remember all the good things about hanging out with Levi and Elsa. Levi tells funny jokes that you never expect to come out of his mouth, and Elsa lets me be sad if I want to be sad, and Levi's mom is always happy to talk to me about magic.

She's another person who makes me feel not alone.

"Okay," I say. Some days I can have fun with Levi and Elsa and be happy. Not the same. But happy.

Happiness remains too, even if it's different.

"Wanna play tag?" Levi says when we get to his house. Rachel is on the porch. I wave and she waves back.

"Magical Clover," she says when she sees me. "It's a little cold today, kids. Maybe we should all head inside?"

It is colder than it usually is in Florida. It has been cold for a few days, colder than I've ever known it to be here. Vermont cold. I think of Danny and scarves and the fireplace and hot chocolate. I think of Glen and Isabelle and hope and apple cider doughnuts.

Even though it hurts, I love the cold and I love those memories.

I have on the coat Dad bought me on our way up north. My nose stings a little and my toes too.

Yep, this is what it was like in Vermont. I hug myself.

"Just a little tag first," Levi says, and Rachel laughs and says yes, of course, a little tag first.

The temperature keeps dropping. Tag's hard to play when everyone's limbs are frozen and don't want to move.

We play tag with our hands in our pockets, tagging each other with elbows and running to the porch when Rachel brings out extra layers and hats and even mittens that she has from when she was at the clinic herself so many years ago. I think I'm going to have to call this kind of tag Winter Tag, and I'll introduce it to Jake. He'll love it.

"Danny loved to play tag," I say when we're all out of breath but determined to keep running.

Elsa and Levi stop. I almost never talk to them about Danny. I keep all my feelings and memories locked up inside, like I'll lose them if they get out.

It feels okay, though, talking about it now. It doesn't make me feel any further away from him. But it does make Elsa and Levi feel closer to me. I'm so surprised, sometimes, by how things feel now that Danny's gone.

"Well, we better keep playing then," Elsa says. Rachel doesn't stay outside with us, but she watches from the window and it's nice, being watched by her. I don't know who's winning at tag, but we're getting sloppier and sloppier and chillier and chillier. My shoulders keep shimmying all on their own, without any direction from me. They shimmy and shake, and my legs too.

The cold is giving me an excited feeling, like something wonderful might happen. I'm nervous-excited, and my heart beats harder than usual.

"Break!" Levi says. He sits down. Elsa sits down too.

I stay standing. I jump up and down a little, bounce on my toes to stay warm. But I don't want to go inside.

I get a warm feeling in my chest and all over. My outsides are still shivering and numb, but my insides are heating up.

I know this feeling. It's my old Danny feeling, the one I've been searching for. I can't explain it to Levi and Elsa, but I smile at them and they smile back and don't bug me about sitting down or ask me what I'm doing, staring at the sky and grinning.

It happens.

It starts to snow.

I take a deep breath, and my lungs are cold with the air and warm with the connected-to-Danny feeling at the same time. It's wondrous.

The snow lands on my hair and my eyelashes and my neck. It's cold and wet and white and everything Danny and I imagined it would be.

It's snow, in Florida.

It's never snowed here, not in my whole life and probably not in my parents' whole lives either. I can't stop looking up. It's coming down faster than I imagined, and more softly. It's magical. It doesn't seem possible that the world creates this for us. Danny would have loved it.

Maybe Danny's the one who created it. I don't know. Even with all that science, I don't know every single thing about how the world works.

I smile, like Danny and I have a brand-new secret. I didn't think we'd ever have a secret together again.

"So beautiful," Elsa says.

"Ridiculous," Levi says, and that's true too.

I don't say anything. But I feel the tiniest bit less sad, the littlest bit healed.

The magic, the thing between me and Danny, isn't gone forever. And snow isn't impossible, even here. I stick out my tongue. The snow tastes a lot like water, but more delicious because it is unexpected and gentle and rare.

No one predicted snow would happen today. Not even the weather forecasters. It will be all over the news for the next week at least. They'll tell us all the times it's snowed in Florida and talk about cold fronts and air pressure and condensation and other fancy science words that I'll like to learn about, but those words won't be enough to explain the swirly, twirly patterns the flakes make on their way to earth.

Some things don't make any sense, no matter how much research you do. Some things just are.

No one knows why it's snowing.

No one but me.

ACKNOWLEDGMENTS

Sometimes it takes time to find the heart of a book, and with this book it took the thoughtful, wise, inspiring feedback of my editors, Katherine Tegen and Alex Arnold. Katherine and Alex, thank you for giving me the guidance I needed to tell the story I wanted to tell. You added so much depth to this book, and I'm incredibly grateful we got to work on it together.

Thank you always to my agent, Victoria Marini. You're there in every book I write, adding clarity and love and layers.

I've been so lucky to work with the incredible team at Katherine Tegen Books. Thank you for the support you've given my work and the time and love you've put into help-ing my books find readers. Thank you especially to Rosanne Romanello, Alana Whitman, Amy Ryan, Aurora Parla-greco, Bethany Reis, and Valerie Shea. And thank you to Emma Yarlett for your beautiful illustration.

Very special thank-yous to my writer friends who gave feedback along the way. Danny and Clover needed a lot of love and insight, from the first few pages to its final revision, and this author needed a lot of encouragement and focus. Kristen Kittscher, Claire Legrand, Caroline Carlson, Elisa-beth Dahl, Brandy Colbert, and Jess Verdi: thank you for the time you gave and the words you said. Your thoughts were invaluable and your encouragement is priceless.

Thank you, Kaitlin Ward, Brandon Millett, and Sandy Chisholm for helping me with some research aspects of the book. Thank you for sharing little bits of your life with me.

As always, thank you to my family, old and new, and my friends who are like family.

As this is a book about a boy and a girl who are best friends, a special shout-out to two guys who taught me a little about the magic of boy-girl friendships: Mike Mraz and Mark Souza.

And thank you, Frank Scallon, for always being there.

Read on for a sneak peek
of *Corey Ann Haydu*'s next
magical middle grade novel
EVENTOWN...

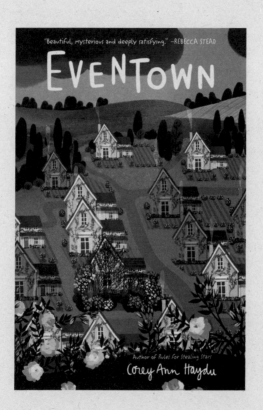

1

Jenny Horowitz likes horses and the color pink and asking lots of questions about things I don't want to talk about. Today she's got one of her favorite horse T-shirts on, a pink one, and she's asking me about The Move, even though every time she mentions it I turn to Naomi and ask a question about multiplying fractions, which we're learning about in math class. Jenny, Bess, and Flora should all know that if I'm talking about multiplying fractions, I must *really* not want to talk about The Move.

Of the two of us, Naomi is the harder twin to read. I love talking, but she's quiet all the time—when she's happy or sad or scared or anything else. I can see the little differences.

When she's happy she blushes, and when she's sad she stares out windows, and when she's scared she leans in close to me, like I might protect her.

And I would. I would try to protect Naomi from just about anything.

I'm just not so sure who's going to protect *me* when we're in our new town.

"Do you think the other kids will like you?" Jenny asks. "Are the kids different there? Mom says everything's different there."

"What's one-fifth times two-fifths?" I ask my identical twin sister. Naomi shrugs even though I'd bet anything she knows the answer. She looks up at the ceiling and crosses her arms. She is angry, but no one else can tell.

When I'm angry, everyone knows it.

And I'm starting to get angry right now.

Naomi sees it and gives me a look that reminds me to act normal. Naomi and I have found that if you act normal when you're out in public, you can save all your sad and sorry and worried feelings for home.

At home, when it's just us, we do a lot of being sad and sorry and worried.

But at school Naomi is That Amazing Gymnast and I am The Girl Who Makes Weird Cookies and we are both in The Group of Girls Who Most People Pretty Much Like.

Lately, though, I've been having a harder time pretending to be The Girl Who Most People Pretty Much Like (Even Though She's a Little Loud and a Little Weird Sometimes). I know I'm supposed to be Elodee from Before and Naomi is supposed to be Naomi from Before, because otherwise we have to be something much, much worse.

Still, it's hard to be from Before when you are in Now. I am not doing the best job at it. Last week, I yelled at Jon in the middle of English class. I used a bad word. One of the only words Dad says we can't use. I said it right in front of the teacher.

I got in trouble of course, but Jon did, too, because everyone heard what he said to me. It was something very, very mean.

It made Naomi sad. Things that make me angry often make Naomi sad, and that's the part of twins no one really understands. Especially me.

"Why are you moving in March?" Jenny asks. "Shouldn't you wait until the summer and move then?"

"What about dividing fractions?" I ask Naomi. "Is that even harder than multiplying?"

Naomi nods. "Dividing is really hard," she says. She looks out a window and I know the sentence has made her sad. I wish she could get angry with me instead.

"Have you even seen your new house? Have your *parents*

even seen it? Don't you have to see a house before you move into it?" Jenny is relentless. She's speaking so loudly that other people are turning and looking at us, and no amount of shushing from Bess or nudging from Flora seems to be stopping her.

"Fractions are weird. I like regular full numbers better," I say.

"Me too," Naomi says. I'm running out of things to say about multiplying fractions, and I'm hot under my arms and all over my chest.

Flora and Bess are exchanging glances that they think I don't notice, but I do. I notice the way they roll their eyes at the weird things I do, and the way they sometimes lean away from me like they don't want other, more popular girls, more normal girls, to know that we are friends.

What they don't know is that I don't care about any of that anymore.

What they don't know is that it's Jenny who is being awful by not stopping her question asking when I obviously don't want to answer. I am angry at all of them with their tiny, almost-invisible dismissals and the not-so-tiny ways they tell us that they want everything to go back to the way it was before, not because they want us to be less sad, but because they want their own lives to be easier.

Sometimes I'm so angry at my friends I wonder if I even

have room for other things like sadness and happiness anymore.

I wonder why Jenny can't see it, simmering under my skin. Pricking my eyes, making me sweat.

"I heard my mom talking to my dad, and she says it's really good you guys are leaving and you should have left right away because your family really needs a fresh start so that you can be okay again and leaving here is the best way for you to do that."

It happens so fast, I could almost pretend it didn't happen at all.

I shove Jenny Horowitz against the wall. My hands press hard into her shoulders, my elbows bend, and I let it all go—The Move, the last few months, Jenny's stupid horse shirt, the fact that Naomi's a gymnastics star and I can't do a cartwheel, Bess's birthday party last month where she invited Flora and Jenny to sleep over but didn't ask me and Naomi, the way my shoes pinch because I need a new pair and Mom keeps forgetting, Dad's bad moods, Jenny's incessant questions, the way people say the words *fresh start* and how it sounds more like a threat or a punishment than some great goal to work toward, Naomi's quietness getting even quieter, and everything else that's made the last few months feel like something I'm carrying around and not something I'm moving through.

With all that going into the push, it's a wonder Jenny doesn't fly right through the wall, into the janitor's closet on the other side.

Instead, her glasses—pink, of course—fall from her face, and her shoulders meet the wall with a thump, and the other kids around us gasp, their hands over their mouths and their eyes moon-wide, like cartoon characters instead of real people.

It takes about one second for Ms. Marley to rush to the scene, as if she knew something like this was going to happen.

I didn't know, though. I never seem to know what's coming.

It didn't feel good, hitting Jenny. It didn't feel good calling Jon the bad word, either. It felt inevitable, though.

Sometimes I think feelings are bigger than people. More powerful. They make people do things that can't be undone. I used to think feelings were part of a person, but lately I've been thinking they are separate beings, that they come like aliens and invade people's bodies and cause destruction.

Naomi didn't agree or disagree when I told her my theory. But I heard her sniffling in the top bunk later that night, and I thought, *Yep, there's an alien, taking over Naomi's body for the night. What a jerk.*

After hitting Jenny, I sit in the principal's office and

make fists with my hands and keep all my muscles very, very tense. Sometimes I hang my head and take deep breaths, but I don't cry and I don't yell and I definitely don't shove anyone else.

The principal doesn't get mad at me. She doesn't punish me since it's my last day of school anyway.

I have always liked the principal. She wears dresses with cat patterns and bird patterns and giraffe patterns, and she makes goofy jokes that kids make fun of but I sort of like. She has never treated me any differently than she did last year.

"Some days are harder than other days," she says with a sigh, like she knows the same things I know, like she's shoved someone, too, like she's sat in a little room like this one and gotten a headache from the effort of trying to be okay. "Isn't that right, Miss Lively?"

I don't say anything. I don't make any noise at all. But I nod at the way a principal in a dress covered in elephants can say something so simple and so true.

2

The next morning, our last full day in Juniper, I help Dad in the yard with the rosebush.

The rosebush is the prettiest thing in all of Juniper. It might be one of the only truly pretty things here, in fact. Bess thinks the glass elevator at the mall is pretty and Flora thinks the skyscrapers we can see from the highway are pretty and Jenny thinks the big white houses in the center of town are pretty, but I'm not so sure about any of that.

"Are there roses where we're going?" I ask Dad while he grunts and digs and gently touches the reddest petals.

"You remember," he says. "There are roses everywhere in Eventown. You said it was prettier than Juniper could ever be. You're the one who said you wanted to live there."

I do remember. I remember everything, because when something happens I turn it over and over and over in my head a thousand times until I am sure I understand it. And sometimes I make a cake or a cookie or even a pot roast based on the thing that happened. When Mom got her new job offer with Eventown tourism, I made a celebration vanilla cake with confetti sprinkles on top but a confused strawberry-raspberry-peanut-butter center. When I called Jon the bad word, I made apology cookies with bitter coffee bits inside. When Bess "forgot" to invite us to sleep over after her party, I made spicy, angry pasta with lots of chili pepper and even a dash of Tabasco in the sauce and jalapeño bread instead of garlic bread. For dessert I made the sweetest chocolate pudding with the fluffiest marshmallow whipped cream because Dad said even the angriest days can have sweet moments.

"If there are so many rosebushes there, why do we have to bring this one with us?" I ask. I love this rosebush, but I also feel a little sad about taking away the only pretty thing in Juniper. Once this rosebush is gone, the prettiest thing in Juniper will probably be the pond over by Flora's house, but it's an ugly brown color and slimy when you stick your feet in. I always look for goldfish in there—a flash of orange would make the pond so much nicer. But there are only ever tadpoles.

"It's the family rosebush," Dad says. "We can't leave

without it." He's sweating onto the handle of his shovel, onto the ground, onto his shoes. From inside, Mom and Naomi watch, Mom shaking her head and Naomi with the look on her face that she's had for weeks—like she's thinking too hard but no thoughts are coming.

I have my own shovel and a pair of gloves Dad gave me for Christmas. I don't love gardening and dirt the way he does, but I like the smell of flowers and grass and the way Dad's face relaxes when he's out here, his worried eyes un-worrying themselves, his fists turning back into regular hands.

Plus, I have to be extra-helpful after the Jenny Incident. When Mom and Dad got off the phone with the principal, they didn't punish me or yell at me or even talk to me about what had happened. Mom sighed and handed me a cardboard box and told me to start packing up the kitchen. Dad said he'd need help in the garden. I, of course, didn't argue with either of them.

Still, it's strange to do something so big and not get in any trouble for it. Lately everything Naomi and I do is okay. Even when what we do really, really isn't okay. Parents and teachers and all the adults in Juniper seem nervous around us. Like it would be dangerous to get too mad at us.

Even Mom and Dad don't have much to say to us anymore. It feels like there's a list of things we aren't supposed to talk about or even think about or feel, and I'm trying my hardest not to talk or think about any of them. Not even with Naomi. Not even with myself.

But it's not easy.

It's uncomfortable, like the whole world tilted just the tiniest bit to the right and gravity and all the other laws of the universe aren't working quite right anymore.

The world did tilt, I guess.

We almost fell off the edge, I think.

I shiver, not wanting to think about tilting worlds or the principal's sad-pitying-nervous face.

I gesture at Naomi to come outside, waving my hands. Naomi sticks her tongue out at me. I stick my tongue out at her. She gets a look on her face that's filled with mischief, and before the look fades, she disappears below the window frame. A moment later, her feet are in the window, dancing and wiggling in the air.

It makes me laugh.

In the midst of everything, Naomi can still make me laugh. She turns herself back around, and when her face is back in sight, it's red and beaming.

"Your turn," she mouths. This is the Naomi no one else really sees. She doesn't like other people seeing that she's goofy and silly and funny. She keeps it all locked up, and I'm the person who gets to see it.

Still, I wish I had someone to be silly with out in the world.

I put my hands on the ground and fling my feet in the air. They fling themselves right back down. It hurts and I'm muddy and grass stained, but Naomi's laughing and I'm laughing and it's a joke that no one else thinks is funny but us.

Which makes it the best kind of joke there is.

Every once in a while, Naomi and I make each other laugh, and it almost feels like everything might be okay again someday.

Maybe in Eventown, it will be.

ALSO BY
COREY ANN HAYDU

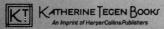